THROUGH HER EYES

NJ MOSS

BLOODHOUND
— BOOKS —

www.bloodhoundbooks.com

Print ISBN: 978-1-5040-8293-8

PART 1

"Half of the time I don't know what they're talking about; their jokes seem to relate to a past that everyone but me has shared. I'm a foreigner in the world and I don't understand the language."
— *Jean Webster*

CHAPTER ONE

I once made a comment at a burn-victim support group, about how ruined we all were – sobs were making my voice crack, so melodramatically, as if their pain was lesser than mine – and they all hated me for it. It was the only time I attended: shortly before I fled the remnants of my regular life.

They were right to hate me. Who am I to brand them with that?

But I'm allowed an opinion of myself. I know what other people see: the desert-like landscape of my face, dunes of scars, or maybe that's pretentious metaphor bullshit.

Maybe that's the wannabe novelist – the failed novelist. The half-successful journalist.

Now, I stare into the mirror, and a ghoul stares back at me. People can say anything they want, but that's what I see.

My mind does unfair things, bringing the old me into being, a mask over my real face. I see the wide brown eyes and the smile and my skin that sunburned so easily.

Ha, *burned*. Goddamn it.

I'm crying again, my eyes stinging.

I should know better. It was years ago.

I have a motorhome and money; it's easy to disappear through England, interacting only when I have to. I'm not running from anything. Which is a lie, obviously. I am running. I'm not sure where.

I, I, I... *I* am sick of myself.

Other people interest me. They are a window into a different reality, one that has nothing to do with flames or rage or pain. Or maybe it does, but that's fine. It's not *mine*.

This is how I end up parked down the street in a mid-level neighbourhood. These are the sorts which have big houses, big gardens, but also a sense of hunger; some of the owners are reaching above their pay cheques, and others are bravely pulling themselves all teeth and guts into this upper-middle class world.

Driving through here last week, this very neighbourhood on the outskirts of Bristol, the house looked appealing to me; it has a metal fence surrounding it, but it's short. The walkway appeared to be crumbling slightly. The door had a ramshackle look about it. There were no visible alarms.

The house is big, a juicy-looking thing, bursting with secrets.

As I turn the corner, approaching my objective, I think about my other prizes.

I've seen sex, lovemaking – two different things – and so much more: casual acts of affection, of cruelty, a family saying goodbye to their dog, a proposal, a tense conversation after which a wife left her wedding ring on the table.

It's like journalism, but only for me. I don't write it down. I document it all in my mind, little pieces of these people.

The fence is easy enough to climb. Despite my general otherness, I take pride in keeping a fit body. I never used to, back when I was carefree and young and didn't know how evil the world could be.

Hopping down from the fence, I stalk across the large garden. No security light blinks on.

There are lights on in the house; it's late, almost midnight, but the three downstairs lights scream yellow.

The wind brushes against my face.

It has become socially acceptable to wear a mask in England ever since the pandemic, and that helps me: I can cover half my face, pull a hat down low, and nobody notices or cares. Not that I enjoy it.

But here, there is no mask. Just the wind and my purpose.

I kneel near the bushes, short of a pool of kitchen light. I can see the sink from a side view, and partially the doorway beyond it. As still as a patient spider, webless in the dark, I wait; I'm not sure how long, and I know I may get nothing tonight.

But then a noise reaches me: *slap*, and a breath.

Moving closer, all I can hear is the *slap-slap-slap*. The breathing – if there was any; I'm not suggesting they're dead, but I mean, the loudness of it – it's gone.

A pause.

I'm holding *my* breath, that's for bloody sure. I'm smiling and I don't know why; the situation doesn't sound good. It's so real, so human.

This is private, their home life. Oh, God, this is good. And bad. And everything in between. I'm hurting with trying to figure out how to feel.

A man appears in the doorway. He looks like a banker, a lawyer, something like that. Shirt and jacket and big chunky hands and a crude twist to his lips.

He swaggers nastily over to the sink, washing his hands; I see his knuckles, how bloody they are, like he's been hitting something over and over.

Slap-slap-slap.

I hate him. It's so clear what he's done.

As he washes his hands, he stares down at them, his expression turned away from me.

His face: I need to see it, to see the evil there, the hate. I *hate him.*

A woman enters. She's so thin it's noticeable, with sharp cheeks. Younger than him, her blonde hair is messy. She glances at the man, then walks out of view.

I can't help but see Maisie in her, like I can save her. Is it that scar near her lip, similar to the one Maisie had, a little crescent kiss?

A voice raised; the window is cracked, and I lean in oh-so eagerly. "Do you want a cup of tea?"

The man pauses in his handwashing. It's so grim and I cannot look away. Maybe even if God offered me a new face. My eyes are locked on the way he pauses, gazing down at his soapy blood-flecked knuckles. I cannot see the hands now, but I did, and I know how they must look.

"Yes, thank you."

Out of view, the frail woman boils the kettle.

I wonder at her injuries. His knuckles were bloody, but her face was unmarked. Her dress had been baggy, going all the way down to her knees; it had long sleeves. It could cover up any number of places. And since she's so thin, he would be punching bone in places: bloodying his knuckles on his own wife.

Men like that deserve a bullet in the head. They deserve to have *other* men, bigger and scarier ones, crash through their bedroom at night: drunk and leering and cheering and swaying, and telling them, *Get up, get up, you know what to do.* Then these men do terrible things, non-consensual acts, and the man knows how it feels.

"Do you want a cup of tea?" I whisper, mimicking the woman's deadened voice.

It's a risk, but they're out of view. I recede into the darkness.

After moving position, I can watch as they sit at the table, sipping from their mugs, saying little.

The woman smiles; the man nods.

That's what people don't understand. Or some people: maybe most.

It's the casual aftermath. It's the non-event of it. It's the cup of tea, the placative smile aimed at the beast; it's the film you watch that night, frozen next to the monster, wondering if he'll awake again.

Once the lights go out, I leave, walking down the street. The house tries to pull me back. There's something more here: more than the proposals and arguments and life-ness I witnessed before.

Their lives are already partly mine. I rarely return, not after I've seen something significant.

But I need more.

My name is Jessica, by the way. I like to imagine I'm talking to somebody: a silent listener. I like to remind the silent listening something, or perhaps just me, that I'm a real person, with a real name.

Jessica Victoria Langdale, one-time journalist, presently wraith of the night.

I'm returning to that house. Tomorrow.

CHAPTER TWO

Every month, I transfer money from my savings into my spending account. I'm not extraordinarily wealthy, but I'm richer than wandering the streets at night, scanning the pavement for cigarette butts, simply so I don't have to walk into a shop and buy some tobacco; even with the mask, the lights are too bright, the stares too inquisitive.

It's worse when I chance to run into a drunk person. Or an arsehole. Or somebody who's lost an argument and wants to take their anger out on a stranger. It's rare – mostly people are awkward and kind, in my experience.

What happened to your face, love...

Nothing happened to my fucking face but something will fucking happen to your fucking face if you keep staring at me like that.

Obviously I never say this. Meekly, I stalk away.

I have a pack of fifty rolling papers, purchased several months ago (with me cringing beneath the glare of the twenty-four-hour petrol station light). I've got twenty-three remaining. I'm not a huge smoker – anymore – but something about the scene in the magic house, the secret-scented house, makes me need the nicotine, the horrible and lovely taste of smoke on my tongue.

Once I've gathered up ten or so butts, I jog back to the motorhome, using cardio to fight some of the negative effects of the smoke.

Sitting on a foldout chair, I smoke the harsh tobacco. The stars glisten down at me from a clear sky; horrible memories touch me, like when *he* curled his arm around my shoulder and whispered he loved me, that he wished he could kiss me for every star in the sky. And look here: Jessica is giggling, laying her cheek against his chest, smiling like a fool.

Come hither, kind sir, and clasp me in your cursed chains.

Is that from a half-remembered poem, or is that my wannabe artist shit again?

The nicotine makes my head rush.

Stumbling inside, I collapse onto the bed, drawing my knees to my chest and pressing my eyes shut. This will be my place for hours, until either I slip into unconsciousness – it never feels like sleep – or the sun rises.

I've got a date in the morning; I don't want to be late.

The husband leaves for work at seven forty-five.

He drives a car that doesn't fit at all with the run-down nature of their home. It's shiny, silver, a proud car for a fiercely capable man. I'm across the street, in a jumpsuit, kneeling next to an internet electrical box.

Experience has taught me that if a person in a work uniform kneels next to one of these, people generally leave them alone.

Pretending to tinker, I watch as the wife beater climbs from his car and walks toward the metal gate.

I can't hear him, but I'm sure I see him sigh, his shoulders bowed, the weight of the world on his oh-so innocent shoulders. It's always the way with men like this; *they're* the wronged party, life is out to get *them*.

He drives the car through the gate, then steps out to close it, all with the same woe-is-me aura around him. It's like he didn't beat his wife ruthlessly last night.

He's hurt his wife many, many times. And yet he has the temerity to sigh.

The cockroach.

After he's gone, I pack up my toolkit – half of which I've got no clue how to use; appearances matter, unfortunately – and return to the motorhome.

Later, I make another pass through the neighbourhood, but the house is quiet. After an hour, I return, and the wife rewards me with a glimpse of her fragile inner world.

She's sitting in the garden on a lawn chair, leaning back, sunglasses on her face.

The property is constructed in such a way it's difficult to delineate between the front and back gardens. The rear of the property opens onto another property, separated by a fence. The house sits centre in the middle of large greenery, much of it wild.

The wife is in what might be called the side garden, as though part of her wants to be seen from the street: wants *me* to see her.

I can't linger for long. I'm a masked and hatted passer-by, nothing more, a Covid-paranoid unburnt pedestrian on their way to a perfectly normal and civilised social engagement.

The wife is wearing a one-piece swimsuit, not a bikini. The day is warm. She's a good-looking woman, with the sort of body

I've never achieved. Lean, magazine-cover looks, but she doesn't want to display her body; she doesn't want to display the bruises.

I know all about that.

The dresses we choose, the make-up we wear – in late-stage bruise development, the latter can sometimes be marginally helpful – the lies we tell, all to hide the purple and blue and yellow tattoos on our skin.

I didn't mean it, babe. I never mean it.

Maybe you need to know precisely what happened to me, silent listener.

So here it is, in as much detail as I can muster.

Here is what happened to me.

CHAPTER THREE

J essica was always interested in other people.
    Jessica studied journalism at university.
    Jessica made friends.

Jessica met Kurk, and she was infatuated by his name. What a cute and unique name. How funny that is; let's laugh and banter and fall in love over a name.

And they did that: fell in love. Or so Jessica thought.

Jessica secured a job at a newspaper. She was a better journalist than she thought she'd be. Kurk, after dropping out of university, became a failed salesman, then a failed get-rich-quick guru, then a failed nothing. He managed to contain his anger to rants and cupboard-breaking for a time.

Then Jessica got pregnant; the pregnancy led her to agree to his proposal, though she wasn't sure she wanted to marry him.

Jessica gave birth to Maisie, the cutest, funniest, most creative, most loving, precocious and sublime and brilliant and perfect girl who's ever lived.

Kurk got angry when Jessica wouldn't let him hurt Maisie, so he hurt Jessica instead.

Jessica mustered her courage and asked for a divorce.

Kurk said no.

She pressed, and The Night happened.

The Night was when Kurk locked Jessica and Maisie in their respective bedrooms and set fire to the house. The Night was when Jessica, after almost shattering her hands to bash her door open, wailed and screamed and hammered her fists on her daughter's door, but realised something was blocking it.

The Night was when Kurk died, Maisie died, and Jessica lived.

The Night was when Jessica fled the house; her primal instincts taking over, she would later tell herself, and she ran. There was no other choice.

The Night was when Jessica stopped thinking of herself as a person.

Or thinking at all if she could help it.

CHAPTER FOUR

This is the longest I've remained in one place since The Night. Well, I mean, since I was able to leave the hospital, arrange my affairs, and disappear. I'm not missing or anything; my friends know where I am through infrequent emails.

I'm simply gone.

But now, apparently, I'm found. This crumbling house with all its secrets holds me in place.

Since I'm staying here for a time, I stock up on supplies at a twenty-four-hour supermarket. These places are my salvation. Sometimes, I can feel the employees staring at me, as though debating asking me to remove my hat. But it rarely happens.

Eyes down, mask on, hat protecting me, I carry the basket to the self-service and scan everything as quickly as I can. I'm shaking as I do it, which is bloody annoying. It's the memories...

Mummy, can I have a chocolate bar, pretty please?

Always so polite, little Maisie, seeming to the rest of the world like any bright-eyed little girl. Do I deserve some pride for the fact I never let him touch her?

No – honestly, I should've left the *first* time he hinted at hurting her.

But that's what it does, the sort of life I lived; it makes the decent thing seem like an extra effort, like I deserve a medal for not letting my husband abuse my child.

Whoop-de-fucking-doo.

As I scan my sanitary towels, a smile causes my mask to tickle my face. Here's something a woman buys, a human breathing person, but that's not me. I'm surprised I even still breathe sometimes.

It's not funny, but I smile all the way out of the shop, a canvas bag-for-life in each hand.

I use a variety of tricks to make passes on the house. There's jogging, which I enjoy anyway. Then there's the drive-by, the walk-by; studying the topography of the neighbourhood on Google Earth, I also learn about a nearby hill which, with the aid of binoculars, will give me a view straight into their garden.

After some research, I purchase the binoculars online, picking them up at a corner shop at midnight, from an automated locker, eyes averted the whole time.

With my new toy, I'm able to watch the couple with more leisure.

There's a tickle at the edge of my mind, telling me to start researching. My laptop is right there; it would be a simple thing, especially with my old journalist contacts. But I'm not sure I'd want to get them involved.

I could at least learn the couple's names, learn where the husband drives to every day. It's a fancy job, I know that much; he always looks like Mr Important when he leaves in his shiny look-at-me car.

If I research, however, I'm crossing a line. Lingering here is already a mistake. Attachment is emotion, and emotion is pain, and pain is death, and here I am sounding like a Jedi. But you get the point.

It seems the couple have purchased this house as a renovation project. They spend two evenings half-heartedly painting the kitchen. Both times, the wife quits; she seems so tired, like all she wants to do is sleep and never wake up. I know that feeling well.

Once she's gone, the husband returns, stares down at the paint; he does this for a long time, like he's catatonic, then he seems to snap awake and pick up the paintbrush. He continues to paint; I think his hand is trembling, though it's hard to be sure. Angry at his lazy wife, his not-good-enough wife, his everything-is-her-fault wife.

After the painting, the husband comes outside, hands on his hips, looking up at his battered home. *A battered home and a battered wife, what an unlucky ducky you are, what a poor soul; you deserve sex on tap and anger on tap and everything on tap, big impressive man. You deserve so much more than this.*

With an up-and-down of his shoulders, he goes inside, as if he's had enough.

I wish I could see through the walls: see what he's going to do to his wife, the redirected sense of failure, of it never being enough, and there she is, the idol of all his ignored sins: a slap, a punch, a fuck. Anything to make her squirm so he doesn't have to.

For Christ's sake. I'm hyperventilating.

I rush through the park, eyes averted despite the sunset, despite the hate, despite the mask.

What if it spiralled to where a passer-by thought they needed to offer me help? What if they saw me?

Beauty lies in acceptance. From ashes we rise. A smile defeats all sadness.

The quotes return to me, the ones on which I binged after

The Night. None of them feel remotely close to true. I was beautiful once; I didn't know it, and neither did very many people, but I was beautiful and now I'm not, and no amount of lying to myself will change reality.

If you weren't so voiceless, silent listener, you might tell me to pull myself together; you might say I don't deserve pity, not after how I failed my daughter. Or you might be one of the sympathetic ones, telling me I have to forgive myself, every day is a new day, one step at a time, blah-blah-blah.

None of it matters.

All that matters is later, I'm back in the park, on the hill, and the night is murky. Sunset has gone. I'm alone except for some other person's wordless drunken wailing from the other end, a laugh: glass and metal sounds I can't quite identify.

Through the binoculars, I watch. The only thing which gives me hope is the light in the kitchen.

Maybe they're not asleep yet; maybe *she* never sleeps, statue-still next to him, praying he won't wake up...

I watch. I don't think, not about *me* anyway.

Finally, when I'm close to giving up, there's movement. The wife runs through the kitchen, toward the back door. She throws it open and stumbles out, face turned up to the sky; her mouth opens in a scream, as if she's letting out all the heartache. The husband is at the door, waving his hands, clearly imploring with her to get inside.

Do you want to make me look like a prick in front of the neighbours?

But I can't hear the words.

She finally stops screaming, deflates; turning to him, her shoulders shift. He stops waving his hands.

"Leave," I whisper.

When she returns to the house, he closes the door behind

her. The lights go off, making it seem like the house is blinking out of existence.

How can I leave?

But also, really, how can I stay?

It's not like I can save her. She's nobody to me, probably nobody to most people, even those who know her. Her situation is being repeated all over the country, the world.

Man seeking vulnerable woman. Must be willing to endure psychological and physical abuse for years, decades, for her whole life, however long that ends up being.

"I can't save her," I mutter. "I. Can't. Save. Her."

CHAPTER FIVE

It's time for some journalism, if basic internet research can be given such a lofty title.

I have their address; that gives me their names. That leads to several mentions online, the most interesting being the husband's employment page. He's a lawyer at a flashy firm, their offices overlooking the city, trendy and modern and elite and nothing at all like their sad decaying home.

Patrick William Hemsworth. And the wife is Anne Hemsworth. Her Facebook page tells me she's thirty-five; he's fifty-one. Her photo makes her look younger, all bright-eyed and smiley.

Anne is a tragic figure online, everything seeming fake, forced. But then how can I judge that when I've seen the truth? I could never have a fair frame of reference. It was like when I was out in public with Kurk, fake smile making my cheeks hurt, and I wanted to scream, *Can't you see what he really is? Can't you see how miserable I am?*

But I didn't. Then The Night happened, so I should stop whining really.

There's only so much the internet can tell me. There would

be only so much a private investigator could too. Hiring one is an idea I've had, but what can he tell me that I can't find out for myself? Plus, it involves somebody else, an extra Nosey Nelly who'd take some of the... not *fun*, but some of the uniqueness, some of the... not *thrill*, exactly, but something.

They'd take some of the something away from it.

But people talk to strangers, if the stranger can play it right. I've done it countless times. A look across the bar, a subtle nod, and the person is spilling it all out: lines and lines of juicy copy spewing from their absent-minded lips. And I'm there, speaking in all the right places, gesturing, a gold-star conversationalist, a beauty, completely unaware of how special this gift is.

I tear away the scarf and toss it to the ground.

The motorhome door is propped open, the mirror letting me see myself and the flashes of the city beyond. I'm truly pathetic, my clean cheap clothes – I don't need nice things – fitting my form snugly. My mask covers most of my lower face, but I'm puckered around the eyes, visible despite the shade of the hat.

Nobody is spilling their secrets to the Devil. I am Satan. I am unforgivable.

I'm so sorry, Maisie.

I run up and down the motorhome, screaming, making a bloody fool of myself.

How could I be both those people, Kurk's toy and effective at my job? Thank God Kurk was such a financial failure; he was forced to allow me to work, since my job paid so well. But he hated it; he weaponised it endlessly.

"Didn't go the whole way, though, did I?" It's like I return to my voice, dehydrated and raspy. The floor digs into my backbone; I guess I stumbled at some point. My thighs ache. "Miss Confident couldn't get her daughter away."

This is really unfortunate. I'm back in my head, which is bad enough, but I've also made a right mess. The motorhome is a tip. And to make matters more annoying – and painful – I've carved the word *Safe* into my leg.

I haven't done that in a long time, but there it is. I must've blacked out; it happens sometimes, more often than I'd like.

The word sits atop thick healed scars, all saying that same word, the impossible word.

The thing I can't ever be: what a funny joke.

Safe. It's weeping red.

God, I'm sick.

CHAPTER SIX

Through my binoculars, I watch. Something interesting happens.

Three times, a new man comes to the house. It's always in the late afternoon and Anne always looks flustered when she meets him, rushing out and quickly opening the gate. There's lots of hand-waving, as though she's telling him, *You shouldn't come here.*

He's younger than Patrick, wearing sporty clothes, a preppy look about him. He looks like a retired soldier from the way he carries himself, shoulders wide, walking proudly toward the house as if saying, *This and everything in it belongs to me, including this woman.*

A thrill touches me someplace, I don't know where, but there it is, tickling.

Is she having an affair?

I never dared to cross that line, though I was tempted many times. To feel love. *Loved.* Like a woman, like a human. Like more than a mother and something to aim fists and genitals at.

Not me – them.

They remain inside for twenty-three minutes, then he

comes out alone, still with that same stiff walk. His demeanour gives nothing away, but what were they doing in there?

Next time, I'm going to be closer, ready to follow.

Late afternoon, twice this week alone. That means he'll be back. I could rent a car, something more agile. It'll hurt, walking into a dealership, but I'll use all the annoying necessary techniques beforehand, the breathing exercises and stuff, the things I always hate doing because it's like I deserve help.

But I need the car; I can't lumber after him in the motorhome.

I have a plan.

I'm not thinking about myself anymore.

I'm thinking about Anne's lover, and what will happen if Patrick finds out.

CHAPTER SEVEN

I reserve the car in advance online.

I'm in the motorhome, behind the wheel, proper cliché white-knuckling the hell out of my steering wheel, as I stare across the street. It's a walk through the shiny glass frontage, and then up the long rug that makes a walkway to the counter.

There's too much brightness, but they're not open at night.

The weather is offensively good. We're supposed to be in bloody England. It's borderline tropical.

Okay...

I walk, and at some point I'm not really thinking.

The door feels weightless as I push it open. Each footstep becomes a cloud, and I'm not here, like I sometimes used to be not-there when Kurk played his sick games.

It's okay: do what you will with that hunk of skin.

"Excuse me."

I sort of collapse back into my body.

"You have to sign here."

His finger goes tap-tap-tap on a piece of paper. He's not looking at me, so I quickly duck my head and scrawl a signature.

Or a squiggle, really, and then I take the keys and turn, stopping. I don't know where to go.

Which car is it?

I cannot, will not, flatly refuse to have a public panic attack.

My legs carry me; out the door I fall. Then – *poof* – I'm across the street, in the motorhome.

I collapse onto the bed and then it's all the same shit. The same memories. There's Maisie, sweet as a butterfly, flapping her wings as Kurk runs at me with a cutting motion, his arm: sideways, *sharp*, then it's a different sort of pain. How many shades of agony there are. How many hues of sadism.

I'm not sure how long I stay like this.

Let's be honest about it, real blunt. It is unacceptably pathetic for me to let this happen, to collapse so easily into a self-pitying heap. I don't deserve it, not after I ran.

There was no way to get to her and I was almost passing out and there was so much smoke, smouldering. Sometimes, I imagine I carried her out of the house, after the fire had done its work; I imagine...

But I can't. I won't.

Finally, I can sit up and feel a little like myself.

I peel off my mask and quickly wash my face, avoiding the mirror, wondering if I should tape over it again. But that made it difficult to adjust my mask before heading outside; remnants of the black duct tape still cling to the glass, scratched here and there with my nails.

I grab a hoodie, then a new mask and a baseball cap. I pull the cap low and the mask high, then put the hood up. Here I am, a five-foot-six wannabe gangster. Let's go.

A shaky smile touches my lips. I'm safe, apart from my eyes.

The man who served me is standing around the side of the building, smoke rising into the air. My heart skips a little when the wind carries the smell toward me. It reminds me of university parties, of the rare times I would go out with my journalist friends, the fresh scent of weed on a balcony.

The man looks up, and right away I pull my sunglasses from my hoodie pocket and put them on. I realise too late how strange that must seem, this duellist-in-a-western motion.

He's youngish, maybe mid-twenties, with a skin fade haircut and big round glasses. His build is fit, bordering on muscular.

"Are you all right?" he asks.

"Fine. Yes. Thank you."

He laughs lightly, then takes a long pull on his joint. It makes a sweet crisping noise and he blows the smoke out, grinning as it shrouds his face. "Why do I get the feeling you want something from me?"

He's not looking at me; nobody does. At least he's talking to me.

"I need my car," I tell him. "And... well, I have money."

He chuckles again. "You have money."

"Yeah."

"I'm not sure what that means." He takes another drag, sucking it almost down to the end. "Here you go then. If you're saying what I think you are."

"What?" I look around; the road back to my motorhome is empty, but there are cars parked on the sides, and the dealership rental place is all glass, or at least mostly; we're around the corner though. Will anybody see? Will they care?

"How can you smoke that at work?"

He just laughs. My hand tremors as I reach out for it. I'm not only burned on my face, of course. My hand is the same, and I see him wince, for a moment: a second.

But then our hands brush, and he seems to make an extra effort to meet my eye and smile.

I turn away, pulling my mask down so he won't see, quickly bringing the roach to my lips and sucking. I suck it all down, the bitterness of the tobacco mixed in with the sweet kiss of the weed, then keep going, until the ash crisps against the roach.

I almost cough, but I remember uni days, friends laughing in the hazy background. *Don't waste that weed by coughing, Jess.*

I inhale it right down into my lungs, let it linger, then blow it out slowly.

When I turn back, the man's still there. His eyes are far kinder than before. The day is bright, warm. My motorhome is over there; across the street. The man was going to sell me...

No; the end of his joint, we're talking still.

My mask? I pull it up.

"Thank you," I say, trying to focus. "That was very nice of you. Most magnanimous."

The man chuckles. "I'm not going to ask what that means. Right, I need to get back to work."

"How *do* you smoke at work?"

He grins over at me, like he knows a secret I don't. "You've already asked me that."

"I didn't."

"You did. Can I get your number?"

"My... number?"

For the most deranged moment, I think this man is hitting on me.

"Yeah. If you want more of the magical plant that makes you forget questions you just asked. Or you good?"

"No, I want it." To forget, to not have to think; alcohol makes me black out way too easily, and it brings the pain crashing back far too harshly. But *this*... "I have money."

My hand goes for my hoodie. I've got my satchel beneath it, strapped around my body, with my purse and cards in it.

The man steps forward, shaking his head. "Don't give me anything here. Jesus."

I take a step back.

He's bigger than me, wide-shouldered. He looks like he can handle himself.

A phantom fist connects with my face, making me wince.

The man stops, tilting his head, like he thinks my reaction is over the top. "Give me your phone. I'll put my number in. If you're sure you can handle it?"

"I can handle it," I say, assuming he means the weed; I'm not sure I can, though, but it's better than thinking.

"It's your lucky day," he says, as he types in his number. "What's your name, by the way?"

I actually think this is the first person I will have said it to, except for you, silent listener.

My world is still collapsing, as usual, but nowhere near as bad as before. Everything is sort of okay, even if there's disaster at the edges.

"Jess. And yours?"

"Luca. All right. I need to get to it. Do you want an answer to your question, Jess?"

"My question?"

He chuckles. "How stoned are you?"

Very, is the answer.

"I can smoke at work," he says. "Because nobody gives a shit about anything anymore. Everything is going to hell and nobody cares, or everything is all right and nobody cares. You know what I mean?"

I don't have a clue. "Yeah, sure. I need to get my car... I don't know if I can get it now, though."

"We can keep it here for you. It's all good."

"I'll have to go for a walk. Maybe a walk and then I'll get it. It was only one inhale, maybe four seconds, that's it. Less. I should be fine, shouldn't I?"

"There's a park nearby, Jess... sorry, Jess or Jessica?"

Under my mask, I'm beaming.

"Whatever," I say, like it's no big deal, like people ask my preferences all the time.

"Jess then." He shrugs. "There's a park. Have a wander. I'm off work in two hours anyway. I could drive it for you, then get the you-know-what. I'm bloody gasping this month."

"Gasping?"

"For funds. Moola. Goddamn hours at a shitty job I hate."

"I'll do that then. Thank you..." Remembering his name takes some effort. "Luca. But wait."

He pauses, turning to me.

"Will this be okay?" I wave at my face. "At the park?"

I'm not sure why I'm asking him, this man with the big glass eyes, but there's something there, something nicer than everybody else. Maybe it's because he knows my name, or I know I can get more of this from him: this feeling.

Weed's bloody everywhere in this shithole country, Kurk used to rant. *Fucking state of it.*

And sometimes, in my most tragic fantasies, I'd roam the street at night collecting butts, making a blunt, smoking it and forgetting about the things he did to me.

"Will *what* be okay?" Luca looks flustered.

"Me. My face."

"Jesus Christ. Yes."

He walks off, not looking back, and I stare, feeling weirdly analytical.

It's like I don't have to rush on straight away. I can stand here, thinking about what he did, giving a stranger a pull on his joint; he said he was hard up for cash, so maybe that's why. But he was kind too, if a little abrasive.

But then... as I walk, I ask myself, what if this is a trick?

What if he's going to rob me?

But I want the weed; that's the cold fact of it.

I want to do it late at night, when the world is silent, lie in bed and stare up at the ceiling as I listen to music; I want to forget everything, and be in the music, songs from when I was a teenager, from when I didn't know how blessed I was.

I walk down the street, not thinking of where I'm going, hardly wincing at the cars rushing by, counting my breaths with each step.

The sun is out and I'm walking.

CHAPTER EIGHT

"Why are you doing this?" I ask, and I know this is wrong.

It's like I've woken up here. Another blackout.

I'm in the car with the man from the dealership, Luca; he's driving. He's young and handsome and surely has a whole life to be lived, but he's here: casually changing gear as he glances over at me.

"Doing what?"

"Why are you helping me?"

He snorts. "Selling you weed?"

"I'm a stranger."

He looks too closely at me, and my head gets woozy. The world is spinning really far too fast.

"Careful. Not in the bloody car. Fuck."

The car screeches to a halt and my hands scrape for the door handle. It's his voice, the man, deep and terrifying. It's the same as the time I vomited in the car and Kurk leapt at me, and...

And we know what happened, what he did. *We* know, silent listener, listening silently; I'm puking on the concrete, cars whizzing by, my mask around my chin as tears sting my eyes.

It won't let me leave, the memory, locking me in place. Kurk is there, doing what he did. I'm aching and screaming, begging for some release, begging God or fate or whatever the fuck else. Always, every second of every day.

Then the scream becomes Maisie and I can't take it anymore.

I let out a cry, another stream of acid vomit spewing from my guts. My belly cramps and I fall to my side, shudder.

"Jessica? Jess?"

Jess.

Kurk whispered it to me in the beginning, his breath on my neck, and I hate it: hate that I ever enjoyed it. Hate that I was ever fooled.

A hand on my shoulder. I flinch away.

"Jess, please. Relax. You're rolling around in your own sick. Fuck's sake. Come on."

I kick out, but then there are powerful hands under my armpits. Luca drags me to the car, sitting me down. He walks over to the side of the road. It's not as busy as I thought.

We're in the hilly suburbs; no cars are whizzing past. The street is quiet, in fact.

That is not normal. Did I imagine them? That is certainly not normal.

Luca takes a few steps back, reaching into his pocket for a cigarette.

I quickly avert my eyes, pulling my mask up, but there must be some sick on my mouth because it smears all over my lips and cheek. The mask is sticky and warm with it. My sunglasses have fallen off, the world suddenly bright.

Luca sees me looking, walks over, hands me the glasses.

"I thought you were messing around earlier," he says, lighting his cigarette and taking a long drag. "At work. Jess. Were you messing around?"

"Yes," I whisper.

He cocks his head, smirking. "Oh, really? So you remember that we met two weeks ago? I've sold you weed six times since then? You remember all that?"

This could be real. And I've forgotten. Which means I'm more messed up than I thought.

Luca laughs. "That's for almost puking in my car."

Something weird happens. I open my mouth and joy comes out. My belly cramps as I laugh some more, and Luca's laughing; we're doing it together. We meet eyes, or I meet eye and he meets sunglass, and we smile; my vomit-coated lips shift beneath the mask.

"I thought I was going crazy. I blackout sometimes."

I shouldn't tell him this, anything.

"Jesus," he mutters.

"Not a lot," I tell him, no idea if that's true.

I never let myself think about it, the little blips. My mind has to do certain things to survive what happened.

"It's my way of dealing with it, I guess," I say. "Being a monster. A freak. A goddamn fucking *beast* walks up to you when you're smoking a joint, and you offer to sell her weed? To drive her rented car for her?"

Luca sighs. "That's not a very nice way to talk about yourself. You're not any of those things, Jess."

"You saw my face."

"I still think it's a horrible way to talk about yourself. My uncle was the same, when I was little, before the surgeries. He basically raised me, that man. I was never scared of him. I'm not scared of anyone. So the answer is, basically, I'm selling you weed because I need the money and I think maybe you need the help."

I interlock my fingers. "It was nice before. In the park."

Before the blackout. I wonder if I did anything, or simply sat

33

there, a figurine on the bench. But I've never done anything the other times; at least, as far as I know. What are the chances I would start today?

Don't think about it; it doesn't exist. It fades from my mind, bye-bye.

"How much can I get?" I ask.

Luca chuckles. "Wipe the sick off your mouth first. I saw you cringe when you put the mask on."

"I can't."

He stares at me, eyes big in his glasses. But no; wait a second... he's not wearing his glasses anymore.

"Where have your glasses gone?" I ask.

He smiles, his eyes creasing at the corners. "Ha, ha."

I wonder if I should wonder. But *ignore ignore ignore* is an easier tactic: *it never happened* works just as well. Put it to the back of the closet, that ugly outfit you're never going to wear again, shove it back there and pretend it doesn't exist. So why do we hold on to it? Because maybe it will come in useful?

What good can this do?

He had glasses; now he doesn't.

Luca looks closely at me. "I mean it. This isn't a joke."

I wave a hand. "I know. *I* was joking."

"Oh." He narrows his eyes. "Ha."

"You might want to turn away then," I mutter.

"Nope."

With a swallow, I take off the mask. I fold it over and use the clean side to mop at my lips.

I feel Luca's eyes on me, but mine are closed, safely hidden behind the sunglasses. I imagine, in a different life, maybe this being an erotic moment. Or romantic. Or something; he would watch me, captivated by my lips, hungry for them. And I'd know it; I'd tease him. Innocent and fun and so full of life.

But no. Never again. Not for me. And not when I'm wiping sick off my face.

I look around for somewhere to put the mask.

"There are some tissues in the glovebox."

I look around the car properly for the first time.

"This isn't the rental."

"I'm taking you back to the dealership after we sort you, remember."

"Yes," I lie. "This is your car."

"Yeah."

"It's remarkably clean, Luca. Very tidy."

"Thanks. No excuse for a shit tip of a car."

I wrap the mask in tissue and tuck it into my pocket to throw away later. That leaves me with the issue of my face, but Luca doesn't seem bothered. Not that I look at him as he walks around to his side of the car. I mean to say he doesn't shout, or run away, or throw things at me.

"Your uncle..."

"You don't need to worry about your burns or anything. It's all good."

My hands tremble a little as I raise them to my sunglasses. This isn't a good idea. I need to remember I'm broken, but that's woe-is-me shit, oh-I-deserve-pity tripe; it's not real, not true. I have to face this.

The world brightens again when I take off my sunglasses. But I keep my hood up, risking a glance at him.

He looks back at me. There's an adjustment of his eyes, as they take me in, but then it's like he's processed it and it doesn't matter. It's so rare I almost cry.

"So how much?" I ask.

We close the doors and Luca starts the engine. "As much as you want to buy. We're going to my mate's. He's got plenty."

"Do you mind if I bank transfer the money rather than pay in cash? I'm still a little worried about being robbed."

He chuckles. "Yeah, it's all good. But don't worry. I won't let anybody rob you."

CHAPTER NINE

I 'm back to my regular self, back to the Hemsworths.

I decided I wasn't going to use any of Luca's weed until I completed my mission. Then I failed, smoking a little with some tobacco I'd scavenged. It tasted good, made me feel sharper as I trailed the man, Anne's preppy maybe-ex-military lover, down the motorway.

Driving the car while high is scary, but I'm focused, thinking only of the man. He's a few cars ahead of me.

I spotted him leaving the house again, this morning: the morning after Luca looked me in the face. After he took me to his friend's house and sold me fourteen grams of weed.

He's a good person, Luca is. He seems like it.

So did Kurk.

It was luck, the man coming today. I refuse to pass on the chance.

His car is bright red, easy to spot, but this is still putting me on edge. It must be the school holidays. There are kids in all the cars, wrestling and laughing and Maisie-like, making me remember flame-hot memories.

The man switches lane; he's going to Weston-super-Mare, the nearby seaside town.

He turns; the traffic, there's too much.

Fuck.

I miss the exit. His bright red car drives away; he disappears.

I'm back to thinking about other people, sitting in the motorhome, smoking and sitting in the smoke. I find myself wishing Luca was here, somebody to talk it through with.

But that's a silly thought. He was friendly to me. Nice. Fine. But that doesn't mean he wants to *talk*.

And if he did, I couldn't discuss this with him.

An idea. What am I thinking, racing down the motorway? It's easier than that.

Plan: buy a tracking device on the internet, using a service that delivers to lockers. Pick it up. Place it on the car.

Wait. Watch. Follow.

CHAPTER TEN

A fter picking up the tracking device, I watch Anne's house from my usual spot in the park. Three days later – three days of peaceful winds and soft sunshine and waiting for my chance – the man appears again, this time in the afternoon.

I jump in my car, feeling a rush like my old journalism days, my heart fluttering, but also feeling calmer.

I've been high all day every day. My emotions are quieter; everything is more distant, more manageable. Though I do notice a sense of something terrible coming, as if taunting from the edges of this new mood; I ignore this feeling as fiercely as I ignore so much else.

I drive down and park up, rushing down the street. I don't want to seem suspicious, but I've got no clue how long he's going to be in there.

The tracker works by securing to the car and recording all of its movements. Later, I'll need to come by and pick it up, transferring the data to my computer. Then I'll be able to see what sort of man dear Anne is getting involved with.

At his car, I pull the I-need-to-tie-my-shoe-laces trick, quickly placing the tracker above the wheel.

I spend the next couple of days smoking, watching, waiting.

There's a special kind of beauty in having a purpose this clear. The rest of life slips to the sides, pushed away on verdant green waves.

Once he's back – two days; he can't get enough of her – I sneak to his car and collect the device.

Once I have his address, I study it on my laptop.

He lives in Weston-super-Mare, on the hill overlooking the seafront. On Google Earth, I study it, the upscale exterior, the hanging plants.

Before I drive to Weston, I wait for Patrick to return home. I wait for the lights to click off in the old dying house. And like an assassin I stalk through the dark, over the fence, and affix the tracker to his car.

The radio plays. Luca's smile flits across my mind, an unfair thing. The mask is cloying around my face, the hat making my head sweat. Sweat flecks the glasses. I'm baking in this car, taking intermittent sucks from the pipe: another online purchase, delivered at the same time as the tracker.

You're blasting through your supply so you can see Luca again. A not-very-helpful voice laughs in my head. *You want that man. You want him to want you.*

I drive, drive, then I'm here, outside the house. It's been repainted since the Google Earth photo. The front curtains are open; the man's in there, in a polo shirt, one hand resting on a beer. He has his knee crossed over, wearing chinos, staring at a TV. A woman sits next to him, her hand in his.

Waiting, I watch, can't look away. Tingling all over. Alight with it, the regular beauty of it. This man is cheating on his wife, girlfriend, whoever she is. He's a pig.

And yet this is so beautiful, the simplicity of life.

So he's with this woman, but he keeps visiting Anne. Twice this week. Keeps going there. Keeps returning. Anne is seeking something in him he already has: the emotional connection, the security of a home. Perhaps this man is using her for sex. It wouldn't be surprising. It's a common enough occurrence.

I tug at the things covering my face: the mask and the glasses and the hat. A glimpse of reflection shows in the rear-view mirror, and I wince, but I'm alone in my car and–

A mother and her child, closer than I realised, walking by me to get to another car. The mother is on her phone, wearing a steel-blue tracksuit. The girl turns, looks up at me; I stare down, instinct making me open my mouth to say hello.

The girl screeches.

The mother looks up at me, and her face twists agonisingly. Civility kicks in a second later, but there's still fear in her eyes. "Sorry," she mumbles, tugging on her daughter's hand. "I'm so sorry."

"It's okay," I say, though she can't hear me; she's already gone, rushing down the street. "It's really okay. It's all right. I don't mind."

Starting the car, I decide to leave this for today. I've done enough. I'm crying, but there's nothing new there, Jessica the master of self-pity. I hate it, how quickly tears spring to my eyes.

Emotions aren't as distant as I thought, apparently.

Another suck of the pipe as I drive, smoke dancing around me. I wish there was a whole cloud of it, filling the car, masking everything.

Anne, sweet Anne – your man isn't *your* man. He's using you. Or he's lying to you. He's not going to leave her. He's going to string you along for as long as you let him.

And if Patrick finds out...

I wince in remembered suffering. The suddenness of

violence, the sheer animal fact of it. Never believing, not for a second, escape is possible.

CHAPTER ELEVEN

I make a few passes of Patrick's workplace, masked up this time, while a rap song plays on repeat from my speaker system. I've always liked all kinds of music, the same way I enjoy all genres of books. It's the thing I care about, the substance of it, not what it belongs to.

The song is called '*Mask Off*', and it repeats the phrase over and over, making me smile as I try to sing along. It's something I'm not going to be doing today: not again. Not after what happened with the girl.

Mask *on*, more like.

The lobby to Patrick's office is wide and clean-looking and shiny, the sort of place I can never go. There's a long alleyway on one side, with the bins, connecting to another big office building.

Waiting for time to pass – playing a bubble-popping game that would've seemed absurd before my head was a haze of weed smoke – I return in the late afternoon.

Parking up, I walk around on foot, exploring the exterior. I've got a big bin bag and a litter-picking stick. People won't question my presence, won't see me, as I skirt around the edges of the building.

There's another area near the back, a bike shed, a few people smoking.

Patrick's there, a cigarette in his hand, looking off into the distance.

I pass him by, head lowered, peeking out of the corner of my sunglasses. The other smokers are heading inside. He's standing there alone.

I bet I could get my car around here: hit him. Drag him inside. Take him someplace. Warn this Kurk-like bastard he can't ever touch a woman. If he thinks about it, I'll end him. I'll make him pay.

He keeps smoking, his hand rising and falling mechanically, as I round the corner, pausing for one last look. He stares down at the cigarette as the smoke curls. I've never seen him smoke at the house, but then he rarely hangs around outside; Anne does, in her recliner, but only when Patrick isn't home.

Tossing the butt, his chest heaves. He walks back toward the office building.

An idea is formulating.

I said I can't save her, but what else am I going to do? My purpose seems so much greater with the drug, the fuel swelling inside of me. I've got a chance most people will never get or would be too blind to see if they did. The chance to help.

I'll need to properly think about this.

Back in the motorhome, I pack the pipe. I've blasted through so much.

At least ten grams. I need to buy a microscale online; then I can weigh it, ration myself, but the feeling is so much better. My mind is so much sharper. I feel like I'm on high alert, yet comfortable with altering my plans, as if nothing unseen or seen can wobble me.

Ignoring, of course, the whispers at the edge of my mind, telling me I'm hammering something which will eventually completely shatter. Ignoring the fogginess which grips me each morning. Ignoring the fact I check the door's locked at least twenty times, then twenty-one just to be safe.

But not me, Patrick...

I could bring him here, to the motorhome. Duct tape, rope, a knife or a screwdriver or something to threaten him with.

All of this can be purchased online. We live in a world of ultimate convenience.

Patrick's going to see what happens when I stop watching, when I take action. Perhaps that will be my future: a guardian angel. A saviour.

I'm flying, floating through the sky. I'm soaring.

Hello, Maisie. I'm going to make it all better.

She beams, radiant, shining with sun bursts, as we glide high above the earth and all its problems.

CHAPTER TWELVE

"What have you been doing?" Luca asks, leaning up against the side of the house.

It's his friend's house, the same as last time, and like last time Luca isn't forcing me to go inside. He's smoking a cigarette, looking young and handsome and very unburnt. He's got a soft smile on his lips as he asks the question, making me think of what *he's* been doing.

"Nothing much," I lie. "What about you?"

I was right; his smile widens. "Seeing Korey, mostly."

"Korey. Your girlfriend?"

Luca shrugs. "Not sure I'd go that far."

For a truly depraved, dreamlike, unfair and unearned moment, it's like I'm his lover spitting his other lover's name out. It's like I'm not some untouchable strange thing. Tolerate me, he can do that, but to be with me. To want me. To think of me as I've thought of him these past few days.

No, obviously not.

"You caned that," Luca says. "Same again?"

"Yes," I murmur, though I wonder if I should get more.

But that would mean not seeing Luca as often. Which doesn't matter, because nothing can ever happen.

"You enjoying it? This is a sativa-dominant strain."

"What does that mean?" I ask.

"Sativa and indica, it's the two types of weed, basically. Sativa gets you going. Energises you, I guess. It's good for creativity. Indica is calmer, can lock you to the sofa, makes you want to chill out."

"I prefer sativa, then," I say. "I'm enjoying things that would've seemed silly to me a few weeks ago. Like this bubble popper game on my phone. I'm up to level three hundred and twelve."

Luca grins, meeting my eye. I've made a special point not to wear my mask, though technically somebody else could see us. It's intoxicating, when Luca looks at me, when he only flinches for the barest beat. And even those are shrinking, as if he's seeing *Jess* when he looks at me, not *burnt lady*.

"That's awesome. Well done. Shall we do this then?"

I shrug; he seems in a rush. That doesn't matter. We're not friends, not properly.

"Same account as last time?" I ask, as he passes the transparent bag of thick green nuggets to me.

"Yeah. But you didn't have to send that extra."

"It's fine. I don't mind. I have too much money, honestly, far more than I deserve. I'm lucky."

Back in the car, I pack my pipe, since I obliterated what I had today.

Driving's easier after that; I glide back to my resting spot like a vampire returning gracefully to her coffin.

In the motorhome: my tools are laid out on the table. There are two rolls of extra-strength duct tape, a Stanley knife, thick black leather gloves, zip-ties, a hammer and a BB gun. The BB gun was the most difficult to get hold of, since it involved actually walking into the shop. I don't really remember the purchase, honestly, only the dizziness; then I was gone.

I turn, looking down at the chair, placed in the middle of the motorhome. It's where wife-beating Patrick will sit, immobilised, feeling as trapped and helpless as Anne, as me, as women all over the world.

"You don't get to do any fucking thing you want," I growl at the Patrick-phantom, the Shade-of-Kurk. The outline of all the bad things ever done to me. "There are consequences. If you ever hurt your wife again, I'm going to hurt you badly, Patrick. I'll break your bones. I'll tear off your fingernails. I'll force you to watch as I set your hand *on fire*."

I lurch forward, kicking the chair, wincing when my bare foot connects with the wood.

Fucking hell. I'm jumping around the bloody place, cursing and ouching.

Laughter comes from me, and for a second I expect Maisie to start laughing with me.

CHAPTER THIRTEEN

I t's an easy task to retrieve the device from Patrick's car. It means I'll have more intel, as they say in the military; I'll be able to plan my mission more effectively. I cradle the unit to my chest as I walk quickly up the hill, breathing the night air hard, no mask on my face to block the chill.

Finally, I transfer the data to my laptop.

Patrick goes home and to work. Also the supermarket, the GP, a takeaway. Nothing strange so far. I move forward on the timeline, spotting an abnormality, a line going far outside his usual path. I type in the address.

How predictable.

Maeve's Massages.

It says it offers "massages", but one glance at the website tells me what it really is. A fuck palace, a cum-swap factory. Perhaps I'm a bit stuck-up in that way: my distaste for prostitution, the profession, not the women caught up in it.

I dial the number, sitting up in bed, preparing to put on my man voice. It's not very good, but people, in general, will accept what they hear. And these days nobody ever wants to offend, which makes it easier for phone calls like these.

"Good morning, Maeve's Massages, Laura speaking, how can I help?"

"Yes, hello, Laura," I say. "I'm wondering what sort of services you provide."

"We do everything above board. All our rates are posted online."

"I didn't ask you if you did anything above board. I asked what services you provided."

"Anything you want," the lady says. "Our girls are clean, enthusiastic, and always aim to please."

This is too much.

"You're making it sound like they're aspiring business-women or scientists or something."

I've dropped the fake voice.

"I..." Laura trails off.

There's so much I want to tell her.

You see, Laura – I want to say – a woman can become a prostitute in her own marriage; her husband is her only client, and he pays her with things. Sometimes a moment of kindness, sometimes fleeting control over her finances. And sometimes, if you give the dirty John what he wants, really do all the depraved things he demands, then maybe he won't hit you that night.

"I'm sorry," I say. "I shouldn't have spoken to you like that. I'm sure you run a fine establishment and do the best by your girls."

A note of pride enters her voice. "I do."

I hang up, deciding I'll visit tomorrow.

But in the meantime, Luca isn't answering his texts. My little magic box of weed is getting woefully low. Soon I'll have to go without for a little bit, maybe a few hours or as long as a day.

I can't afford that right now, not with all the things I've got planned.

"Why have you rung me fifteen times?"

I'm sitting up in bed, trying my best to be patient, but honestly not liking Luca's tone at all. "Because you didn't answer."

He laughs humourlessly. "I was busy. I had stuff to do. What is it?"

"What do you think?" I say, trying for a light-hearted tone.

"Already?" His voice is low. "Jess, maybe you should–"

"There's a way to order it online. I've been doing research. I made an account on the website. It's easy. I'll have to get it delivered to a PO Box, but that's fine; the packages are sealed, smellproof. There are countless reviews."

"I know. I'm familiar."

"So don't lord it over me then," I snap, safe behind the phone. But what if he hurts me next time he sees me? But Luca wouldn't; let's risk it. Take a little chance. "Or I'll find a way to punish you."

He laughs, lighter this time. "Take it easy. All right. Checkmate, you got me. I need your massively inflated rates. Are you feeling okay though?"

"Fine. I'm enjoying it. That's all. Got the money and the time, so what's the problem?"

"True, true," he says absent-mindedly. I can hear a woman's voice in the background, *Korey*, the little love of his little life. "I can meet you tomorrow..."

"Tonight," I say flatly.

Korey pipes up in the background. *"Why can't she wait?"*

"The Bitcoin price is slightly up at the moment," I say loudly. "But even so, I'd still be paying twenty-seven per cent less than I pay you, for the same amount. And it may be higher quality too."

"Yeah, yeah," Luca says. I smirk as I imagine him waving a hand at Korey. "That's fine. Come by the house at eight?"

"That sounds great. Thank you very much."

With time to spare, I decide to have a little nap. The motorhome isn't parked in the best position, behind what seems like an abandoned and derelict pharmacy.

I go to the window, looking out, wondering if anybody saw me or can smell the smoke.

This isn't paranoia, I tell myself. This isn't worsening the splintering of my splintered mind.

The car park is empty. It's late afternoon. The rest of the world is busy living their lives, not hanging around meaninglessly on the outskirts of the city.

CHAPTER FOURTEEN

The rain hammers against the roof of the rental car, properly *slamming* against it. It's so incessant, over and over. I'm waiting for Luca to text me.

My phone rings, lighting up on the dashboard. The world is dark, the phone bright. I imagine my face lighting up; I'm not wearing my hood or mask or anything. I'm sitting outside Luca's friend's house: Dylan, I remember. I'm waiting for my sweet green medicine.

"Hello."

"Do you want to come inside?" Luca asks. "We're waiting for it to be delivered."

"Delivered?"

"Dylan's mate is coming by on a moped. Do you want to come in or not?"

"How long until this friend shows up?"

"Half an hour. Maybe a little longer."

"I'll wait in here," I say, thinking of the walk up to the house, then inside, then the voices of people. I know there's at least one person in there except for Luca – Dylan – but what if there are more?

"Really," I go on. "You should deliver it to me, since I'm paying extra. This is ridiculous."

"Stops you having to go to the PO Box though, doesn't it? Stops you having to see people?"

His words sting, like he's reading my mind, probing at my tenderest parts. "It's nothing to do with that."

Luca makes a grunting noise. I'm not sure what. A laugh or something else. "Fair enough. The door's unlocked if you change your mind."

"I won't."

But he's already hung up, not hearing the last part. I'm sort of glad he didn't hear it. Things are getting far too combative between us, and I need to keep this relationship peaceful. It's true, what he said about the PO Box; I don't want to do that.

And it's more than that. It's him. Luca, because he doesn't wince, turn away, cry out.

I study the door of the house, knowing the old Jess would've done it. I would've sprung in there with my hair all wet from the rain, laughing away any nervousness.

That was always the way, the two sides of me: so seemingly confident in certain situations, when the circumstances would allow me to pretend, to play journalist. But then other times, I was shrunken, hardly a person.

Social bravery isn't for me. Like these silly thoughts of Luca are not for me.

Flames and rage and Patrick's bloody scalp, the dream made reality, those are mine. Nothing else.

And yet my hand is twitching for the car's door handle, the same way it twitches for the pipe: the empty pipe, not even any resin left. Nothing but ash.

Like Maisie. *Ha,* I wish I was dead.

My hand moves to the door handle. And I wonder.

Could I do this? Could I go in there and say hello and then maybe sit down and quietly listen to their conversation?

Luca's in there, at least, a friendly face. I'm doing it. I'm pushing the door handle.

My hand snaps back. I forgot.

Sorting everything quickly – mask, cap, hood – I climb from the car. The only thing I don't wear is my sunglasses, since it's getting dark. I rush across the street, glad for the lukewarm downpour, driving me on.

Up the two steps, I push the door open, sucking in a breath as I stumble along the hallway. I'm aware this is very melodramatic of me, but I can't help it.

It feels so wrong, the trainers in the hallway, the coats on the rack, a hoodie strewn across the hall. All this regular life.

Voices come from what I presume is the living room.

It's a man's house, it looks like, with no feminine touches, no flowers, no bright pictures. It smells a little musky as I take a few steps, the rain sluicing from me.

"Is that your mate?" A voice raised. He sounds like he's from London. "Tell her with her shoes, man."

"Yeah." Luca raises his voice. "Jess, is that you?"

I lick my lips under the mask, my pulse shimmering. "Y-yes."

"Take your shoes off, please."

"Um, okay."

I kick them off, the comfortable trainers. Kurk used to like it when I wore heels around the house, enjoying the fact it hurt my feet; he'd make me choose between walking like that or some other punishment.

Back up the hallway, I turn to the left. Two sagging leather sofas are sprawled out along each wall. The low glass coffee table is covered with snacks and drinks and grinders and papers and a big glass bong, video game controllers and wrappers.

Luca sits on one sofa, a controller in his hand, staring at a large wall-mounted TV.

The other man sits across the room, staring ahead. He's lean and looks younger than Luca, wearing a hoodie and a cap, like me. He's got a tattoo on the back of his hand, an incredibly ugly one that seems like it's supposed to be a woman's face.

It's all mangled.

It's me. Is it there? I blink; it doesn't move. What a stupid question to ask. Of course it's there.

"Dylan, this is Jess."

Dylan nods briefly. "All right."

"Hello," I say, a thrill rioting through me when he looks at me then straight back to the TV with no pause or visible discomfort. "You still stressed about Covid or what?"

"Dyl, she's the woman I told you about."

Dylan looks again. His face is shadowed beneath his hat. *There* it is, the hazy picture of shock, but it changes after a second. "Ah, my bad. But you don't need to mask if you don't want it."

"I'm fine, thank you."

Dylan shrugs and leans forward, resting his elbows on his knees.

"Sit down, Jess," Luca says, indicating the spot next to him.

He's wearing gym gear, I realise, a tight blue T-shirt and jogging bottoms. His arms are thick and strong, the sort of protective arms that would've made a mouse of Kurk. His hair is swept to the side, all messy, making me want to... But that doesn't matter.

There's a definite odour of weed in the air. I can see lots of it on the table, tasty nuggets. I force myself to stare at the TV. I'm a little concerned by how badly I want to leap on the table, grab a butt from the ashtray, light it, smoke it, taste it.

People say it's non-addictive, right? I'm sure I've heard people say that.

Pausing the game, Dylan starts rolling a king-skin joint, spreading out the tobacco. "Luca tells me you're the biggest smoker in the Southwest, Jess."

I laugh, not sure where to look. "I don't think so. Probably not."

"I told him I pack more in one joint than she smokes all week," Dylan says, then laughs very loudly like he's told the funniest joke. "We can smoke this one still. Boy should be here soon."

"Is it the same bloke?" Luca asks.

Dylan grabs his grinder. He must've already prepared some. He unscrews the bottom and taps it carefully into the joint, moving up and down with skill.

After rolling, he smiles softly, handing it over. "Go on then, let's see the pro at work."

"I'm not sure I..."

Luca's hand is on my arm. He's looking at me kindly, with something like real affection in his eyes. He knows why I'm hesitating; I'll have to lower my mask. "It's okay, Jess."

I swallow, taking strength from him, then reach up and pull my mask down. Dylan doesn't look at me; I can tell he's purposefully avoiding it. But he doesn't cringe as I take the joint.

Picking up a lighter from the table, I light and inhale, sucking tobacco in with the weed. It's harsh, far more potent than from the pipe, but I keep sucking. It's been hours since I ran out.

It goes down so nicely, right to the back of my throat, then further, until it's moving through me.

"Thank you," I whisper, blowing the smoke out and handing it back.

He takes it. "No drama."

"So how did you two meet?" I ask a minute later, as Luca takes a drag of the joint.

Despite the problems – the flits of memory, flirts with paranoia – accepting this room, these people, having a conversation is far easier with the smoke bolstering me.

"We go to the same gym," Luca says, handing the joint to Dylan. "Basically, I kick Dylan's arse every week."

"You wish, man."

"You do martial arts?" I ask.

"Yeah. Boxing when I was a kid. Now I do MMA. We both do."

I think of Luca's hard body coming up against Patrick, of the bloody knuckles, of what a pathetically easy effort it would be.

But how could I get him to do it? I wonder what he'd do if I told him the truth, about the abuse, about a woman so scared of her husband she rarely leaves her house.

"Are you any good?" I ask.

Luca grins over at Dylan. "What'd you think, mate?"

Dylan smiles, shaking his head. "Yeah, you're all right. Still slacking with your footwork though."

I smile along with them, stunned at how regular this feels, as I put that idea to the back of my mind: One day, I might be able to get Luca to hurt Patrick.

Or better. Kill him.

But that can be plan B in case my mission goes wrong. Which it won't.

I'm ready.

Look what I did here, overcoming my fears. Conquering them.

Patrick doesn't stand a chance.

CHAPTER FIFTEEN

The brothel – the one my tracker told me Patrick likes to visit – sits on a grimy street, a phone repair shop on one side and a corner shop on the other, separated by a short alleyway. Its frontage is dirty. I can't imagine walking in there with the intention of purchasing a woman.

Patrick is here, his shiny car parked out front, practically begging to be vandalised.

The sun is setting, the day after I saw Luca, after meeting Dylan. Another friend, even if he winced, even if I could tell I made him a little uncomfortable.

My mind wanders to Patrick, to the acts he's committing. What sort of depraved, sickening things is he making those women do? Perhaps she is stronger than I was, and there's a definite *no*, a place where she won't take anymore. That's where these poor women come in.

I pack my pipe, watching, waiting.

Men come and go. Most of them look average, a demographic sweep of the general population, the postman and the student and the builder and a pensioner. There's nothing that marks them out as perverts, except for their presence here.

Finally, Patrick emerges. He's parked his car on the road, so I probably won't get a chance tonight. I was hoping he'd leave it by the alleyway, for some reason: hoped perhaps it was a regular thoroughfare.

But then Patrick turns, ignoring his car. He's walking down the street. His head is held high, his arms swinging fast at his sides, like he wants to get away from here as quickly as possible: away from what he did. So why leave his car?

The sun hasn't set, not completely, and there are people on the streets. Some of them are rough, criminals, drug dealers. But not like Luca and Dylan drug dealers; these look like young feral men eager to prove themselves with senseless violence.

Patrick is getting away.

I make sure my screwdriver is tucked into my pocket, then climb from the car.

Mask glasses hat hood.

The check complete, I'm striding after him, my hands stuffed in my pockets and my head aimed down. I'm not sure if anybody looks at me. I don't look at them.

Patrick crosses the street, turning right. I pick up my pace.

There's a dingy park at the end, behind a gate which swings on its hinges, the lock presumably broken.

Patrick walks to the nearest bench, sits down – heavily – and stares straight ahead. It makes my job difficult. I thought he was going to keep walking, and I'm already in the park now, just the two of us.

Patrick doesn't look at me. Seeming somehow shrunken in his suit, he clasps his hands as though in prayer and keeps staring. It reminds me of the way Kurk would look sometimes, when he said sorry, and I truly believed he meant it.

But he couldn't; he didn't have it in his DNA, his bones, his soul.

I walk to the other end of the small park, taking out my phone and staring meaninglessly down at it.

Nothing's happening, when I feel like everything should be.

There's nobody nearby. The park is deserted. I could act here... and then what? If I knock him unconscious, how will I move him to my car? What if he wakes up as I'm dragging him there? And surely somebody will see; I'm realising, far too late, there are massive shotgun blasts in my plan.

But *look* at him: so full of self-pity, gazing off into the distance, probably thinking about how difficult his life is. Like I haven't seen blood all over his knuckles. Like I haven't seen how calm he is about abusing his own wife.

Like I haven't seen the fear in Anne's face, the acceptance.

I have to do something.

I'm walking over to him, my hand shaking as I reach into my pocket, as I curl my hand around the screwdriver. Something has to happen: perhaps a fright, something to jolt him out of his unfair certainty. The supreme self-belief of the abuser.

I hate woe-is-me shit when *I* do it, let alone when some undeserving bully does. He's been to a hooker, paid to have sex, and he wants to come here and borderline cry about it.

Before I plan it, I'm standing close to him.

Or as close as I can get. My feet won't let me go the rest of the way. It's like there's an invisible barrier around him, because I know what this man can do. *I'm alone in a park with a violent man.*

It's like I'm suddenly sober. What the fuck am I doing?

Patrick finally sees me. He doesn't look as nasty as I expected. But they never do. It's silly to expect it, really.

"Can I help you?" he says.

My voice seizes. My hand is in my pocket, wrapped around the handle of the screwdriver, but I can't pull it out. It's like his hand is already around my wrist, holding tightly, not letting me.

I almost scream with the effort of freeing myself. But nobody is trapping me, except for me.

You can't keep getting away with it. You're going to kill her one day.

His eyes narrow. He looks at my sunglasses, at the exposed flesh between them and my mask. He makes a judgement. He thinks I'm crazy, some weird outcast wandering lunatic.

"Are you all right?"

Don't you ask me that.

My throat closes more. This isn't how it was supposed to go at all.

I shake my head, staring at Patrick, remembering the way he looked when he was washing his hands. His wife's blood. He's a monster.

And that's the thing. I've got no way to defeat monsters. Thinking I did was fantasy. It all comes crumbling down as we stare at each other.

"I don't have any money," he says.

I don't need anything from you.

I walk out of the park. Hating myself with each step, I almost run to the rental car, mind brimming with all the ways that *could've* gone, all the things I *could've* done.

Could... He *could* break my bones, cut, torture me. He could do any number of destructive things. There's no point trying.

That leaves a question. What am I going to do about Patrick?

Luca.

The answer comes, singing through my mind.

Luca Luca Luca.

My Luca.

CHAPTER SIXTEEN

PATRICK

Patrick stared after the figure, wondering what that had all been about.

His thoughts were troubled. She'd just stared in the darkness. He thought *she* because of her build, the way she'd walked. It had reminded him of Anne for one confusing second. Standing there all bunched up, ready to do something, ready to fight.

He laughed bitterly, rising to his feet.

It was visiting the massage parlour. It always depressed him. It always reminded him of the direction his life had taken, of how powerless he was.

The name alone was ridiculous. *Maeve's Massages*, as if that was what they did there: as if everybody didn't know the truth. The figure was gone; she'd disappeared.

Patrick suspected she'd wanted money, perhaps for drugs. It was the same all over the city, but worse in this area.

When he reached his car, he placed his hands on his hips, looking up and down the street. Some bugger had keyed it, on the back above the wheel, a long line; his alarm hadn't gone off.

He needed to get that sorted. Another problem he didn't want to deal with.

He wiped his eyes; it was windy.

Climbing into the car, he sighed and wondered who had done it, who had senselessly keyed his car. After everything, he had to deal with this too.

Was it the figure, the stranger?

Patrick walked toward the big crumbling house, biting down in annoyance.

Anne had said she was going to spend her days renovating it; she was going to hire crews, arrange for everything to be done, or do it herself. They'd agreed on that when they moved in.

But she'd rather lie around all day while he went to work.

He quietly opened the door, taking off his coat, running a hand through his hair.

Life was so cruel sometimes, the turns it took, as if it was planning on making people suffer. It was a mean thing, the stuff a man was forced to endure: the pain and the humiliation, the everyday acceptable misery of it.

He poked his head into the living room.

Anne was on the sofa, wrapped in a blanket, watching TV. Time melted as she smiled. Patrick smiled in return. They shared this, sometimes, these moments: becoming who they once were, before all the horrible things. Patrick knew it was wrong; so did she, he sensed.

"Are you hungry?" she asked. "There's some food in the oven."

"Thanks."

He walked down the hallway, letting out a breath of relief. Maybe she wasn't going to make him do it tonight.

CHAPTER SEVENTEEN

"I want you to ration me," I tell Luca down the phone, the day after the incident in the park.

"Ration you?" he says, yawning. "Do you know what time it is?"

It's seven in the morning.

In the background, *"Luca, who's that?"*

Luca's voice raises, a note of anger. A weird thrill goes through me. "It's my mate. Relax."

Luca walks into a different room, the volume changing. "Are you all right, Jess? This is weird. You have to admit that. You ring me and that's the first thing you say."

"You're weird. A crazy lady came up to you to scab some weed. You decide to be her chauffeur for the evening then become her personal weed pimp."

"I was trying to be nice. And I don't want to be your weed pimp, whatever that means."

I haven't smoked this morning. I feel really short on temper, far more than usual. The prospect of smoking makes me want to sing and cry. I need it and it's the last thing I need.

"I want you to only sell me a certain amount per week," I say.

"Have you been smoking a lot?"

I laugh dryly. "Yeah. And I'm really not supposed to."

"What do you mean?"

It makes me see and forget things and it makes me paranoid and it makes me think I can do anything. I can conquer the world. I can fix the past. What am I saying. I need it.

"My waistline." I chuckle. "I get the munchies big time."

"Oh. You sure that's all it is?"

"I'm sure. But your concern is oh-so sweet."

"Don't get sarky if you want me to *ration* you."

"Will you? I know it will mean less money for you, but–"

"Don't worry about that. I'll... I'll be okay."

"Luca?" Curiosity makes my voice sharp. "Something's wrong."

"Relax."

"I'm right."

"Stop being so bloody persistent."

"But something *is* wrong," I say forcefully. "What is it? Are you okay?"

"Why do you care? I thought I was just your weed pimp."

I say nothing, remembering my journalism days. Not that I was ever some award-winning hard-hitting prodigy or anything like that, but I had my techniques. One of them was to stay silent; people like to talk. It's a cliché with how well known it is, but it's also true.

"I borrowed money for a business last year. It failed."

"How much?"

"Six grand."

"From who?"

"Eh... let's say, the sort of people where six grand becomes fifteen."

"Loan sharks?"

"Yeah, if you want it to sound like a Hollywood film. They're just blokes, mates of Dylan's mates. They're getting pretty mouthy about it. But it's not like you were going to buy fifteen thousand pounds worth of green, was it?"

"No."

"So it makes no difference. The answer's yes, if you need it. I'll ration you."

I think about Patrick: Patrick and Luca, and how the two may be connected. Visions come alive in my mind: Luca's knuckles are red and bloody and cut, and Patrick's face shows the reasons why. *Never touch your wife again. I'll find you, mate. I'll find you and I'll kill you.*

My skin goosepimples as I envision it. It would sound so commanding coming from Luca.

"Thank you," I say after a pause. "What was the business?"

"A fighting gym. We had a trainer, a head coach I guess, one of the best in the country. But then he went and got cancer and died in four months. I was screwed without him."

"I'm sorry."

"It is what it is."

"So you're tough, then. Really. That wasn't talk."

Luca chuckles. I imagine him sitting there in his boxers, his strong body tight. Then he talks to somebody off-phone. *"I'm talking to her. Wait a sec."*

I smile as a tingle moves over my body. It's a rare sensation and I hardly want to admit it, but my... well, my vagina tingles a little. It's that warm fuzzy feeling, the one I haven't felt in a long time, maybe only in my dreams when I can forget who I am.

"What were you saying?" Luca asks.

"About your fighting. You really know what you're doing."

"I'm decent. I'm not the best and not the worst."

"How would you do against a regular man?"

"An untrained person, you mean."

"Yes."

"It wouldn't be pretty."

And there's Patrick: a fist crunching into his face, the flesh making a wet *mulch* noise each time, *mulch-mulch-mulch*, as Luca smashes his skull to pieces.

But no; he wouldn't have to go that far. Simply break his nose. Terrify him.

"Why?" he asks.

"Just wondering," I say, since he doesn't need to know yet.

"All right. Anything else?"

"No. I wanted to make sure the rationing thing was okay."

"It's all good."

"You're too relaxed. You're the most relaxed person I've ever met."

"And that's a bad thing?" Luca laughs. "And anyway, look at you."

"What do you mean?"

"Well, you look like Freddy Kreuger and you still have a laugh, don't you?"

We go into hysterics together. It's a moment completely our own. My belly cramps with how wrong it is, with how nobody else would ever dare to say it. But Luca would, and I can hear in his laughter: it's coming from a good place. It's not mean.

Luca abruptly stops. *"In a minute."*

"I hope I'm not keeping you," I say.

"No, you're not," he replies with a certain manly firmness. "I'm not being funny, but I'm a goddamn adult. If I want to talk to my friend on the phone, I will. If I want to hang out with my mate, I will. You know what I'm saying?"

My hand is doing something very bad. It's snaking down between my legs. Into my knickers. I haven't done this since...

since the start of mine and Kurk's relationship. In *years*. It feels so wrong, as Luca talks.

"I know what you're saying," I whisper, my fingers stroking.

A shudder moves through me. I didn't realise how on-the-edge I was, how quickly my body was going to respond.

"Are you all right, Jess?"

"I'm... I'm sorry."

"Are you... doing something right now?"

Shame touches me and my hand almost stops, but it feels too hot and intense and new.

"I'm sorry," I say.

"Is that a yes?"

"Y... yeah."

"Why?" he asks.

"It feels..."

"Jesus, you're really going for it."

I move my fingers quicker, gasping as the suddenness of the pleasure whisks me up.

Suddenly Luca is in my ear, his voice low like he doesn't want to be overheard, husky.

"Rub your wet pussy quicker, Jess."

"Yes," I whimper, stroking it up and down.

"Is your hole soaked? Is it drenched for me, Jess?"

"Yes," I gasp.

"Finger it. Hard and fast. *Quick*, Jess, you horny thing."

"Jess, are you there?"

This one is reality; none of that was happening, of course. I feel like I've woken up. My underwear is all sticky.

"Yeah."

"I said, I'll talk to you later, all right?"

"Talk to you later, Luca."

I may let you know about a job, I almost add, to keep him interested.

69

He's good at fighting, plus he needs money.
I am not good at fighting; I have money.
It seems so obvious.

CHAPTER EIGHTEEN

ANNE

Anne was lying in the sun, in the garden, like she was in some American film. Like their street was lined with identical houses, with white picket fences and kids playing and happiness everywhere.

But the street was British and mean-looking, because all British streets were. She thought of Nordic slopes, of skis on her feet, of voices lacing the icy air.

She almost smiled; it faded as quickly, and she shifted on the recliner. She couldn't get comfortable. Never could.

It was a hot summer day, glorious. She hated it; she hated the house behind her, the crumbling relic. *A new start.* She should've been painting, arranging, something.

But what was the point? What were they building, really?

She sat up a little, eyes shifting back and forth, safe behind her sunglasses. She didn't like being outside, especially, but she hated being inside. Trapped. Locked away.

There were so many threats in this world, and that was the good thing about this house: the fence, protecting her. She wondered if they could get spikes installed.

That was one positive about Patrick, for all his faults. His *many* faults. Her hands moved over her belly and she shifted in the recliner again. At least he did the shopping, made it so she had minimal contact with the outside world.

Her mobile rang. She bit down on a curse, snatching it from the grass.

Mother.

Anne had initially saved her as *Mum*, but then she'd seen it on a rare visit and changed it to *Mother* herself. Apparently, that mattered. Anne felt tired thinking about talking to her. The phone went quiet, then came alive again a moment later.

Anne tightened her fist around it. She wanted to squeeze, keep squeezing until she crushed it.

Her mum rang three more times. Anne finally swiped answer.

"Yes, hello?"

"Frida," she said, then added *my flower* in Swedish.

Anne cringed. She wasn't anybody's flower, and certainly not her mother's. Anne didn't bother correcting the name. Mum would never accept that Anne had chosen to go by her middle name. Frida was her grandmother's; Anne hated it, or more so that her mother had chosen it.

"Is something wrong?"

"Wrong?" Nadia said. "Why wrong? I want to speak with my daughter. Isn't a mother allowed that?"

As a girl, Anne would grind her teeth whenever she was stressed. When she was in public and there was no outlet, or if she knew showing her true feelings would get her in trouble, she'd bite down and grind and find a release that way.

She never did that anymore, except when talking with Nadia.

Keep sweet keep sweet keep sweet. Screw the Bad Place and screw the video cameras and the red-eyed staring.

"Of course," Anne said.

"How is that big expensive house?"

"It wasn't expensive. It was relatively cheap. It's falling to pieces."

"That would make a fine home, Uriah was telling me. A fine home indeed."

"Uriah," Anne said, not bothering to remember if she'd heard of him before. Nadia was almost sixty but acted like she was in her late teens when it came to men; it was tragic, the power they had over her. "Patrick wants me to do the work myself."

"Well, why not?"

Anne sat up, wincing, more at Nadia's words than anything else. She felt like screaming and she didn't like it, didn't know why; or maybe that was a lie.

Maybe she always knew why she felt like screaming.

"Frida?"

"My name is Anne."

"Why have you not started the work?"

"I'm tired, Mum."

Even to herself, she sounded pathetic. She knew it wasn't the whole truth either. But she couldn't talk to Nadia about her marriage, about any of it. As far as Mum knew, Patrick was a successful man and Anne was his happy wife.

Mum didn't care about the things Patrick forced Anne to do.

"You're tired."

"That's what I said."

"Being tired is no excuse to let a lovely house like that fall to pieces. Is it, Frida? Do you think that makes sense?"

Anne bit down some more, hurting her teeth. She didn't know how to answer her mother's question. There wasn't any explaining it to Nadia. If Anne tried, Nadia was likely to take Patrick's side. It was the way she was wired, always believing other people over her own daughter.

Anne was a ghost: a background figure. A nothing.

"I need to go," she said.

Nadia sighed. "Okay. *Jag älskar dig*, Frida."

"I love you too," Anne said automatically, then hung up.

She went inside and poured herself another drink. Vodka and Coke, a double shot. She had a shot glass to make sure she could measure it all out; she only allowed herself one double-shot drink every hour and a half. It kept her buzzed but not too heavily. In case Patrick came home and started a fight about it. He always said she was more argumentative when she was drunk, but really he wanted to control her.

She drank one glass right there, then realised it didn't really count. She had rationed herself to *sip* one drink every hour and a half, but she had nothing left; she sipped the second one slower as she went outside.

CHAPTER NINETEEN

I have a plan.

It's a plea to his humanity, to *Theo's* humanity.

I googled Anne's boyfriend. I couldn't help it. It was easy enough with his address, leading to the publicly available information, then his set-to-public Facebook page.

In the motorhome, I write a note. I write many notes, but I settle on one.

Theo, you have to do your best to help Anne. I know things are difficult for you. I know you can't tell your partner. You don't want to ruin your life. But Anne desperately needs your help. Get her away from Patrick. If you love her, do the right thing. Please.

I debate signing it *your watchful guardian angel*, but I know that would be a step too far.

Some careful surveillance of Theo tells me his wife never uses his car. It's a simple matter to arrive at his house one morning, ten minutes before he leaves for work, and walk over to the vehicle. I wedge the envelope under one of the windscreen wipers, his name written across the front.

A smarter person would flee once they'd left it.

Sitting in my car down the street, I wait. I watch.

Theo walks out of the house, preppy and handsome as usual. He pauses when he sees the envelope, takes it.

His body grows still, like waves of ice are rushing through him. He looks around, up and down the street. But he doesn't notice me. His hands are shaking. It's like he's working up his courage, building up to doing something, the right thing.

"You can do it, Theo. I know you can."

It won't be much longer, Anne. Your knight in shining armour is coming to save you, like a fairy tale, and I'm the wizard behind everything, orchestrating it all, the music of my vision reaching a crescendo the day Patrick sees what's happened; he's lost. There's nothing he can do, no way he can regain his oh-so important power.

Theo turns to the house, as though to go inside. But then he suddenly spins and paces toward me. He *did* see me.

My hand scrambles for the key. I knock over my box – it was open – and blunts fly all over the passenger seat.

I quickly turn the key and pull the car out.

Theo stands in the street, waving the letter, his voice seeming both very close and far away.

"What is this? What sort of game is this? Did Anne send you?"

She doesn't have the courage. I have to do this for her.

The car carries me safely away. That didn't go as planned, obviously. I didn't want him to see me. But he's got the message. That's why he seemed so angry.

He knows he has to help her. He can't put it off anymore.

Do it, Theo. Do the right thing.

Or you'll make *me* do something drastic.

CHAPTER TWENTY

ANNE

"What are you playing at?" Theo said, sounding wannabe righteous down the phone.

Anne stood at the very rear of their garden. Patrick was in the kitchen with all the lights on. There was a knot in her gut as she watched him walk around, still in his dressing gown, making breakfast.

He'd booked some time off work to help with the house. Anne hated every second of it.

"What do you mean?" Anne said, her voice composed and dignified. She wouldn't let Theo rattle her.

"This note. Apparently I need to *save* you."

Anne laughed quietly. "I don't need saving from anybody."

A pause lengthened between them. Anne paced up and down the grass.

"The note, Anne," Theo said. "Why..."

"*What* note?" she snapped.

Theo did his annoying sighing thing. She could see him there, hands on his hips, looking so concerned. Looking like he cared, like he was ready to hear her side of the story. But nobody truly cared what she felt, what she thought. It was always about them; it always had been.

"The note telling me I need to save you. From Patrick. I have to do the right thing."

"I didn't leave that note."

"Come on…"

"I didn't."

Patrick walked to the window, raised his hand in a wave. He gestured with the frying pan. He was asking her if she wanted bacon. Anne was thinking about her first vodka, but she didn't want a discussion about it with Patrick; she knew too easily where those discussions could lead.

"You didn't send them, him, her? The person? They were wearing a hat, hood, glasses, mask. It was weird. They were watching me, pretending they weren't. Then they drove off when I came over."

"This had nothing to do with me."

"Anne," he said stiffly. "I'm trying my best here. I've been patient. I thought we were working this out."

She raised her voice. "It wasn't me. I don't know what you're talking about. Seriously."

"Are you messing with me?"

Anne ran her hand through her hair, tightened into a fist. She remembered lying in this man's arms, listening to his heartbeat. Thinking – however fleetingly – this might be it. The moment her happiness starts. The point at which she could forget everything that came before.

"It's the truth."

"I don't need this. I've got a life. If this is you, please stop."

"It wasn't. It's not."

"Please, Anne."

"I've moved on, remember. You were the one who found me."

"You know why I did that."

She knew what he *said* about it. But she also knew the truth. He missed her, the same way she sometimes missed him: in her weaker moments, rising from a drunken sleep, hung-over and not really herself. Then she missed him. A little.

"What are you going to do?" she asked.

"I don't know. What *can* I do? Why would this person care about us, or *know* about us? And why the hell would they think you need saving from Patrick?"

Anne thought about Patrick standing at the sink, washing his hands, always the same like a ritual. They'd slipped into it easily over the years.

"She might've seen something. Misinterpret—"

Theo hung up, leaving Anne to bite down on the rest of her sentence. That vindictive asshole.

Anne walked across the garden. Their weirdly shaped garden, like a caricature of a grand estate, their house in the middle and grass all around. She stopped at the fence, looking out at the street, wondering if this masked watcher was out there somewhere.

Patrick walked out onto the porch loudly, causing her to turn.

She could see his too-big smile, as though he wanted to pretend the rest of their marriage didn't exist. He could whittle everything down to this porch, the offer of food.

"Are you hungry?"

She did her best to smile. She wanted to try. They'd had something, once.

"Sure. That sounds nice."

As she ate, she thought about this stranger. It was bad. The note to Theo meant they'd seen him coming to the house. They might have seen other things: events that would shatter her if made public, would make it impossible for her to go anywhere. Not that she went anywhere anyway.

The shame of her very existence.

She couldn't have people *knowing*. She was successful, by many measures. She had a life most people dreamed of.

The perfect house, the perfect marriage, all that horseshit.

PART 2

———

"Poetry is a mirror which makes beautiful that which is distorted."
— *Percy Bysshe Shelley*

CHAPTER TWENTY-ONE

In the motorhome, unsure of the time, I wonder if I should stop smoking. Luca didn't keep to his promise of rationing me. I can't blame him, I tell myself, but I do, a little bit.

I blame myself more. And not just for the endless inhaling and exhaling.

Patrick is so bloody untouchable. It's been two, three... two and a half, something weeks since I left the note on Theo's car. I've relegated my observations from the park at night, binoculars in hand, and it's clear Patrick hasn't moved out.

Suddenly, my phone's in my hand. It's ringing: calling Luca. My joint is smoked right down to the roach.

Time skipped, not for long, but it did, again. Jerking all over the place, leaping about.

Luca answers. "Jess?"

"Hello."

"Uh... you okay?"

"Yes." I lick my dry and hot lips. "How are you doing this evening?"

"It's one in the morning."

"Oh."

NJ MOSS

A pause, and there's a voice in the background. A *female* voice. *"What's going on?"*

"Nothing. Just a friend."

"Who's that?" I ask.

Luca laughs quietly, and I really don't like the sound of it. It's the meanness in the laugh. It's like he's telling me, *You don't have any right to know who I'm in bed with.* My hand clenches into a fist and my temples pulse, right up against my skin, like my forehead is going to rupture. That's melodramatic nonsense, of course, but it's happening all the same.

"Luca?" I say, voice cold.

"It's Tina."

"Tina," I repeat, wishing she was dead.

"Yeah... all right? Anything else?"

"Tina," I say again. "You sure do get around a lot, Luca."

"All right..."

"You do. You seem to be very good at getting women into bed."

My mind's ticking. There's an idea. That's actually a really good idea. And it could work.

Anne is clearly braver than I was, able to overcome her fear of Patrick and risk an affair with Theo. But Theo clearly lacks what it takes to save Anne.

But what if Luca doesn't?

The only thing which would stop me is the idea of him with another woman. But how he behaves! It's shameless. Sickening even, that he'd do this, treat himself and other people like commodities, and not care that somebody might get hurt.

Might have actual feelings, truly care, but oh no, *this* person doesn't have pretty skin and bouncy tits.

"Anything else?" Luca says, ignoring my dig.

"Uh, yeah," I murmur. "I've got a job for you."

The idea makes me want to puke a little.

"A job?"

"Yeah. That's why I rang. Sorry if my banter missed. I'm stoned as hell, Luca, that's the truth."

"It's okay. What's this job?"

There's eagerness in his voice. I showed him my bank balance on my mobile app a few days ago. It touched me when his eyes got all impressed by the number.

It's not a high number, not by the standards of the upper middle, but to a man like Luca, it's all the riches a person could dream of. It also proved something to me: he cares about me enough not to steal from me.

He could kidnap me, force me to withdraw the cash, or transfer it, but he doesn't. Because he cares about me.

"Jess?"

"The job," I say, "is simple. I need you to get another woman into bed."

In the background, this woman. What was her name? Tiffany? Whatever. She says something, *"Luca, I'm trying to sleep."*

This is it, his moment to be a good person. Surely, he's not going to discuss being paid to seduce a woman, not with a woman already sleeping right next to him.

Come down into the gutter with me, Luca. We can do disgusting things down here and nobody's around to judge us for it.

Luca moves to a different room, bed sheets rustling. A door closes. "Tell me about this job."

CHAPTER TWENTY-TWO

ANNE

Anne's life came in moments.

Patrick grunting in the bedroom, staring at her with those hateful eyes.

Patrick washing his hands at the sink.

The cup of tea.

Staring out the window and waiting as time passed, then having some more vodka.

Theo hadn't said anything else about the note. She was starting to wonder if *he* had done it, or at least made it up. But as the weeks passed, she couldn't shake the feeling that something odd was happening.

"Try to keep sweet, little Frida," Mum had said. Many times. "Always with a smile on your face. You must never be rude or petty or unattractive. Come here, let me adjust your bow, what a delicate flower you are; let me use you as a prop when prancing around parties, and never mind if your feet hurt, or bleed, because you know I'll get my way. You know you'll do what I want. Or I'll take you to the Bad Place. Do you want to go there, innocent, delicate Frida?"

Anne sighed as she walked into the garden, trying to push

the memories away. Everything was getting so ugly and over-grown. Patrick said he was too tired from working all day to fully renovate the place; he kept asking her to arrange it.

Anne knew what he was doing: trying to get power over her, trying to *win*. It was always a game with him.

She lay back on the recliner and tried to focus on her book. Reading was the only escape which was still working.

But even that failed; her mind kept wandering.

She wanted to be happy. That was, perhaps, her most fundamental truth.

She didn't enjoy the way her mind lurched, her passion flared, her inability to calm herself down. She didn't like making Patrick angry or upset, causing him to behave in ways which were repulsive to her.

As she sat up, she spotted a young man walking by the fence. He was wearing shorts and a T-shirt, his hair recently cut, a confident smirk on his face. There was something about that smirk, as though he truly didn't care.

She found herself watching him over her Kindle.

He turned his head; he was most certainly returning her gaze. A bizarre yet welcome shiver moved through her. She knew an affair would eventually end badly, but there was some-thing so liberating about the idea of taking another man. Feeling sexy and wanted and not at all like the way Patrick made her feel.

The man suddenly stopped. "Excuse me?"

Anne sat up, caught off guard. "Uh, yes?"

"Sorry, I thought you were looking at me."

Anne faltered. Here was a slice of mayhem, of possibility.

"I wasn't," she said, the only thing which came to mind.

"Oh, really?" He laughed. It was so much better than Patrick's, so much less *forced*. This man wasn't trying to play a role. He seemed utterly himself. "I guess I'm seeing things then. Can you give me some directions? I'm a little lost."

Anne was on her feet, walking across the garden. She noticed the man's eyes move to her legs, to her body in general, and another shiver moved through her. "Where are you trying to go?"

"Oh." The man grinned as she got closer. "Nowhere. I wanted to get you over here."

From anybody else, the line would've made her sneer. But there was something so effortlessly at-ease about the way he said it. It was like he didn't care if she sneered at him, so there was no point. Maybe she'd finally met someone on her level.

"You know," she said, "that sort of talk could frighten a lady."

He leaned close to the metal beams of the fence, not bothering to hide the fact of his roving eyes. She'd thought her looks were failing, with all the drinking, all the doing nothing. But there was proof: a younger man, handsome, with a sophisticated lust in his intelligent eyes.

"Maybe I want to freak you out. What's your name?"

She laughed, but she couldn't let him think she was some ditsy idiot who'd fall for his cheesy lines. But it was the way he said them, as though everything was ironic; life wasn't worth taking seriously.

"Anne. You?"

"Luca." He smiled. "I know this is weird, but the truth is, I'm bored, Anne. So I thought I'd try my luck."

She shook her head. "Does this work often? Yelling at women when they're sitting in their garden?"

"I've never done that before. But I'm a stupidly impulsive person. And, no offence, what was I supposed to do? I mean... *look* at you, Anne."

This was too much, the way he was speaking to her, and yet

part of her thought about asking him inside. It was foolish and she knew Patrick wouldn't like it. But she didn't sense any aggressiveness from Luca: only desire. She wanted the same.

As mad as it was, she wanted to tell him to kiss her, hold her, then take her hard and passionately so she could forget for a little while.

Instead, she turned away. "That's never going to work, Luca. Feel free to try again though."

"I will," he called after her.

With her back turned, she smiled secretly to herself.

CHAPTER TWENTY-THREE

PATRICK

Patrick was at the brothel again. Every time he walked in there, he could've sworn he smelled piss, cum, sweat all mixed together. He didn't like to think about what went on down the corridor in the "massage rooms", especially because he knew Laura had once worked in one.

She was at the desk now, typing on her computer.

Laura looked mostly how Patrick remembered from childhood, down to the colour of her hair, though it was dyed blonde now, not natural. She was still his little sister, with her hopeful smile, breaking his heart every time.

She knows I'm going to say no.

He always did.

"Give me five minutes then we'll grab a coffee?"

"Sure," Patrick said.

He sat in the waiting room, hoping nobody he knew walked in. He always wondered what he'd tell one of his colleagues if he ran into them. He could point the finger back at them; *they* were there too. And for its intended purpose, not to see their sister.

They were there to fuck Patrick's sister, if she'd still been working down the corridor.

Patrick looked down at his hands, at the cuts and bruises on them.

"Shall we get going?"

Laura stood over him, bright, bubbly, as though she thought it was going to be any different. It never was. Nothing ever changed, except for in work, the proudest part of his life. Sometimes he felt like a hamster running on a wheel, waiting for his legs to break so it would all stop.

A man walked down the corridor. Sometimes they were adjusting their belts or looking weirdly proud of themselves. This one was about Patrick's age, wearing a similar-looking suit; Patrick could imagine sitting across from him in a meeting. The man met Patrick's eye, and his lip twitched, a reflexive smile. He was bursting with happiness at what he'd done. Patrick thought about hitting the man.

The siblings went to a nearby café, sitting in the window. From the outside, they were a successful man in a suit and a hippy type with a large hot drink cradled in her hands. Nobody would've guessed how empty they both were. Or maybe they would have.

They chitchatted for a while. Mum and Dad were still dead. Their aunts and uncles were alive, doing fine. Their dogs were doing fine; Patrick thought of Tricksy, his childhood companion, and felt a desperate sense of longing.

On the news went: a cousin had recently announced a date for their wedding. Regular life stuff whirred by, then Laura leaned in; it was the way he knew well. She inclined her head.

"Patrick, I really wouldn't ask..."

And here it came, the part which shattered him.

"I can't," he said.

She frowned, but she recovered quickly. "Why not? I don't understand. You know how much my mortgage is. Mum and Dad are gone. I've got two kids, Patrick, two kids who you hardly ever *see*... You used to help me. I don't understand why you stopped."

I can't explain. Don't ask me that.

"You're not entitled to anything," Patrick snapped, though he knew his bad mood wasn't Laura's fault.

She recoiled. "I never said I was."

"You're acting like it. It's never, *Oh, Patrick, let's have a chat.* It always comes back to this."

"I'm sorry. We're struggling. We really are."

I can't give you any money. I literally cannot.

"Then maybe you shouldn't have kicked Fred out." Patrick was being mean, but it was too late. Anything but being honest with his baby sister. "He had a steady job. He was taking care of you. And you left him... Why?"

"Please," she whispered, looking around. "Calm down."

He sat back in his chair, feeling deflated. "I'm sorry."

"I know it was a silly reason. Or seemed like one."

"No, it wasn't."

Laura had wanted to find herself. That was her reason for ending her marriage with Fred. It had seemed like madness to Patrick. There had been no abuse in their relationship, as far as he knew; Laura never cited it as the reason for ending the marriage, simply this general desire to find out who she really was.

But they'd been happy. And the children had certainly seemed happier back then. At least from what Patrick saw which was, admittedly, not a lot.

"I felt trapped," she said.

Trapped by a beautiful life. And then you started working as a whore. What a smart move, Laura.

He pushed away the nasty thought. She'd royally messed up her life, it was true, but then so had he.

"I know," he said after a pause.

"So you won't help me?"

"I'm sorry, but I've got bills too. I've got a new house. I need money for renovations, upkeep."

"Renovations," she repeated dully. "Upkeep. I'm not sure if I'm going to *have* a house next month. A roof over my children's heads. And you're talking about that."

Patrick stood; this was going in a direction he wanted no part of. "I'm sorry."

He walked away, thinking that would be that. But then Laura's voice rose in the most unhinged way. "You sold your life to that woman. You're an embarrassment."

Patrick paused. The whole café did. Making a fuss was never a good thing, especially in public. He thought about spinning on her, all the things he could say. He could tell her, *"At least I'm not a coward. At least I don't run when things get a tiny bit difficult."*

Instead, he walked to the door, lifted his hand. He stared at the cuts on his knuckles; then he pulled the door open, walking onto the street.

CHAPTER TWENTY-FOUR

"So what did she say?"

"Nothing much, but she was flirty."

"How flirty?"

"Very."

I imagine scraping Anne's eyes out of her head and stuffing them into her mouth, then forcing her to bite down so she could taste them. It's the hitch in Luca's voice.

Then the most profound guilt hits me. It's like I've slapped Maisie across the face.

"You're attracted to her," I say, my hand tight on the phone, the mattress soft against my back, the ceiling spinning.

"Maybe a little," Luca says. "Am I not supposed to be? It'll make this easier."

In the background, Dylan says, *"Man, get it, bro."*

I smile. "Are you playing your game?"

"Yeah, and I'm kicking his arse."

"Then how are you talking to me?" I ask. "Am I on loud-speaker?"

"Nah, I've got a Bluetooth thing."

"Yeah, and you look like a dick," Dylan says, and Luca laughs.

"Putting my money to good use, I see."

"Don't worry. I've already given half to those loan shark bastards. They'll get the rest when I do."

"Good. That's when the job's done."

"Yeah, about that. I don't really know anything."

"Do you have questions?"

A worm of irritation writhes into my skull, squirming about, as though it's going to expand. It's not enough I've given him a godly sum, at least in his terms.

"Why you want me to do it... I guess."

"I can't tell you yet."

I don't *know* yet, but I've got an idea, one that will fuse me and Anne as sisters. I never had one, but Maisie was like a sister to me sometimes – when she wasn't being my naughty wonderful daughter – and I remember the first time I saw Anne, that night which feels so long ago with the haze of smoke and conviction separating us, when I thought she looked similar to Maisie, a girl's face pressing through a woman's skin.

"It's nothing bad," I say. "Don't worry about it. Do what I tell you, and you'll get the rest of the money. Easy."

"All right. But I'm not doing anything illegal."

You might have to, little Luca. And you *will* do it. We both know you will, when it comes down to it, because you're young and scared and handsome and too stupid to realise who you truly belong to. If he'd roared at me down the phone, the night I asked him to do it – what was it; two days ago – and told me, *"I could never do that, Jess, because I want you. I need you."* If he'd done that, I would've ended the plan right there.

But he didn't, so he'll do what I want. For money. And because I'm in control.

Not Kurk and not Patrick and certainly not Luca.

"My husband beat and raped me for years. He burned my house down with my daughter trapped inside. I heard her screaming as she died."

"Jesus, Jess, I didn't mean…"

"So stop whining. Nothing bad has ever happened to you."

But it will, if he carries on. I'm not sure I mean that. I'm not *unsure* either.

"Jess, I…"

"I have to go. Let me know when you make some progress. And later, leave the package on Dylan's doorstep. Okay? I've got stuff to do. Leave it somewhere it won't get stolen."

Luca sighs. "I'll find a place. I'll text you."

I hang up, feeling like something's trying to break free.

"I'm going to save you," I whisper. "I am, I am, I am."

From the ceiling, Maisie stares, smiling with a halo of heavenly light glowing around her innocent face.

CHAPTER TWENTY-FIVE

LUCA

Jess was an odd person, and not only because of the horrible situation which had left her scarred. Luca had actually cried thinking about that the other night; Jess had thrown it in his face the evening she asked him to leave the package outside, but she'd mentioned it before too. She often seemed to forget after, probably due to the weed.

When I pay off these twats, I'm never selling to her again.

As Luca walked down Anne's street, he wondered if that was true.

Jess was bringing him a nice weekly sum of money. She seemed okay, happy enough, spending her days watching videos on her phone, playing games, chilling out. It was a better life than Luca had, in a way, except of course she had to deal with her disability. He remembered the first time he'd seen her face, how terrified she looked.

That was why he'd told her the lie about his scarred uncle. It was a simple thing; this so-called uncle had raised him. Luca hadn't thought about it, had only wanted her to feel better.

She was a good person, from what he could tell, but this job was *weird*.

Luca had a note tucked in his hand. It had been five days since the conversation with Jess. She'd picked up one package since then, but arranged it via text, with the package left in the empty wheelie bin like last time.

She seemed angry, and bizarrely resentful whenever he talked about women. Luca hoped she wasn't getting a crush on him.

The note in his hand read, *If you want to do more than look, reach out.* And then he'd left his phone number.

It was cheesy and he wasn't sure it would work, but he knew Anne was interested. He could tell when he spoke to her, the shine in her eyes, the need for adventure. It was what he always tapped into when talking with women; they seemed to see him as a wild ride, a way to let go.

Luca still had no clue why Jess wanted this, but he couldn't turn down the money. It made him feel dirty, fine, but it was better than broken bones. Or leaving, running someplace else.

The sharks would probably hurt Dylan in that case, or his parents, or his sister. Luca would die if anything happened to Izzy.

Anne seemed to do nothing but lounge around in her overgrown garden. It saddened him as he approached, though he kept his face flirty.

She lay back on a lawn chair with her legs tucked, a Kindle balanced on her knees. The sun was blazing and she really was beautiful, sexy in an older woman way.

"Somebody's relaxing, I see," Luca called over.

"Are you stalking me?" she called back.

Luca laughed, resenting the fact he was being paid for this. He wanted the money, obviously, but Anne seemed nice. Luca wondered how Jess knew her. *This is so fucking weird.* "Oh, yeah." Luca made his voice ironic. "You're all I dream about. Come here a second."

Luca paused at her metal fence, giving him a view of the large property; with a little maintenance, it would be beautiful, like one of those fancy country estates in miniature.

She sat up, her head tilted, a sweet smile on her face. Luca's body stirred as he thought about all the things they could do. "Why?"

He tilted his head, Mr Cocky, though it felt forced. "Because I asked so nicely. I want to give you something."

"Luca..."

"Pretty please?"

There was something so sleazy about this, beyond the inherent dishonesty of it. Even if Luca wasn't being paid, he would've found this slightly depressing. It was how old the house looked, especially contrasted with how bright and attractive Anne was; it was the fact she seemingly had nothing with which to occupy her time. It was the tinge of desperation in her superficially confident smile.

She came over, and Luca leaned against the fence, not trying to hide the way he was eyeing her up and down. He could tell she liked the attention.

He put his hand through the beams of the fence, offering her the note. "Don't read it until I'm gone."

With that, he swaggered away. Oh, he was full of bravado, and he knew she was probably staring after him, feeling romantic, wanted.

He looked over his shoulder, and he was right; she was staring, lips spread into a dangerous sort of smile.

At the end of the road, he did a loop on himself, heading for his car. There were some shops and offices a hundred or so feet up, and maybe that's where Anne assumed he was going when he passed by. Instead, he walked directly parallel to her house, in the opposite direction, down the adjacent street.

Inside his car, he sat back, closed his eyes.

He thought about a bloke Dylan knew, who'd once borrowed money off the same men who held Luca's debt, and what they'd done to him. The beatdown, ten on one, the sort of situation in which no person could defend themselves, trained or not. They'd jump him, use weapons, make it so he couldn't walk again.

Luca drove away from the house, knowing he had to go through with this sick thing. Whatever reasons Jess had, they didn't matter to him. He needed these lunatics to leave him alone.

Then he'd figure out the next step in his life. Maybe he would open a gym one day, but he'd find steady work at one first, or volunteer as a trainer. He'd stop the petty drug dealing, stop hanging around with Dylan's mates. Dylan himself was okay, a good friend.

But Luca could do without all these associates, people recognising him in town as a person who could *sort them out.*

He needed to sort himself out first.

CHAPTER TWENTY-SIX

Maybe you're expecting me to say I'm really the one who burned my house down. I've been having memory problems, so it makes sense, but I assure you that's not the case. I've thought about this very carefully, going over the events minute by minute.

I was sober back then, clear-headed as I could be.

I woke and the house was already on fire. Kurk was ranting, mad, not caring about the flames. Waving his hands at me. And maybe you'll think, *Ah, yes, but perhaps he was pleading with you.* But that's not the case. He was trying to trap me, trying to stop me from saving Maisie.

I want to make this clear because, well, I fear I may have to do some very bad things to make this right. Hopefully Anne allows me to rescue her, but if not, I'll have to take steps to fix the problem myself. We shall see. But as for Maisie and Kurk, it's clear, isn't it, that Maisie was the victim there. But also that I share a piece of the pain, because *he* did it to us, the same way Patrick's doing it to Anne.

The method varies, but the result is always the same. The pain and the humiliation and the feeling it will never end.

So that's cleared up. I'm not going to pull some crazy shit like that on you.

I'm having a few memory problems, fine, but that all started *after* Kurk destroyed my life.

CHAPTER TWENTY-SEVEN

ANNE

Patrick was in the next room; she could hear him cooking in there, banging pots and pans around, acting like he was some kind of bloody master chef. Anne tucked her legs up underneath her, a tingle dancing over her body, as she looked down at her phone.

Luca was saved as *Hairdresser*, but it was not like Patrick ever looked at her phone anyway.

She and Luca been texting for two days. It was so exciting, waiting for her phone to vibrate, glancing at the screen so she could get a snippet of the message in the notification window.

She loved to luxuriate in Luca's words.

I want you so badly.

I can't stop thinking about you.

I want complete control of you.

> I'm going to tie you up like the horny thing you are, spread out on the bed for me, then feast on your wet pussy while you're shivering and moaning and getting closer and closer to an orgasm. Then, when you're close, I'll stop, teasing you...

"Anne, do you want cheese with yours?"

Patrick had to choose *this* moment to interrupt. "No. I'm not hungry."

"I've..." There was that pause, the one he always did, as though he was the world's biggest victim. "I've made dinner."

"I can't magically make myself hungry, can I?"

"Uh... no, I..."

She laughed, mostly to shut him up. She wanted to sink inside a world of Luca, with his savage words and the feelings he triggered in her, making her feel alive for the first time in years. "I'm only joking. I'd love cheese. Thank you so much."

He shuffled around in the kitchen, probably feeling sorry for himself. When he brought the food in on a tray, it was like he was aiming his scabbed cut knuckles at her. She averted her gaze and took the tray, not wanting to look at him, but not wanting to look at the food either. She still felt sick from all the vodka.

"Is it all right?" Patrick asked from across the living room.

She clenched her fist around her phone. She felt like she was going to puke. His tone was so innocent, like he didn't know how loud he was being; it was like he was pretending he'd forgotten all the other times she'd felt ill, and she'd politely asked him to please be a little bit quiet.

But no. He couldn't do anything for her.

"It's fine," she said, picking up her fork. "Thank you."

Her phone buzzed. She glanced at the message.

> I want to see you soon...

A smile touched her lips. Patrick frowned, watching her, but he didn't ask who it was.

―――――――

"This is so exciting," Anne said the following afternoon as Luca drove them through Bristol.

Her jacket was hugging close to her body. She was wearing lingerie underneath it, a shiver moving over her at the danger of it all. The city rushing past. The sun shining joyously down. For once, she felt like herself, whatever that meant. Full of *her*. Able to approach life like an adventure.

"It is." Luca smirked, his desire clear. She could feel it burning from him. "I'm so glad you agreed."

"It's quite an event for me."

"I'm the lucky one."

She moaned as he confidently gripped her thigh, squeezing on it as he changed lanes. He was so in control, stroking his hand up and down, then he laughed and took it away.

"I better stop. You're going to soak my seat."

She laughed loudly, hard, like she hadn't in ages. "That's disgusting."

Luca grinned. "Hey, you're the one doing it, not me."

He took them into the centre of the city, to the hotel he'd booked. From the look and smell of his car – he was definitely a marijuana user – she'd assumed the hotel would be on the cheaper end. None of that mattered anyway; this was about going with the flow, enjoying her life, living *her* story for once.

But the hotel seemed on the expensive side. It had a Victorian look about it, and he led her through the entrance almost like a gentleman, though the pressure of his hand on her back told her how badly he wanted her.

She stood off to the side as he paid for a room. Anne kept

her eyes down, not wanting to look at the receptionist and see the insinuation there.

This was Anne's story, nobody else's.

They rode the elevator up, his hand moving down her back, softly grazing her ass. "You're so hot."

She moved against him, seeking the pleasure, desperate for the sheer physical release of it. It was like they'd rehearsed it beforehand, explaining what they would do to each other.

In the room, they fell upon each other, giving life to the things they'd texted about. As Anne's body rushed closer to an orgasm, her first proper release in years, she knew, with complete certainty, there was nowhere else she'd rather be.

CHAPTER TWENTY-EIGHT

LUCA

Luca lay in bed next to Anne, feeling more than a little dirty about what they'd done. It was how she'd held him toward the end, her gorgeous body pushed up right against his, their eyes locked as they raced toward their shared finish.

It had felt like a real moment, but Luca knew it was rubbish.

"What are you thinking?" she asked, her voice flirty.

Luca rolled over onto his side, propping himself on his elbow. "Mostly about doing that again."

She rolled her eyes, her naked skin marked here and there with red blotches of passion. Otherwise, she was fit and pristine, naked and beautiful. "Such a line."

"Is it a line if it's the truth?" Luca grinned, faking it, forcing it.

"*Is* it the truth?"

"You tell me..."

His hand trailed up her thigh, and for a while, they were lost again.

Luca knew he had to tell her. Jess had specifically asked for it and had paid him a little more cash as an incentive. Luca tried to make himself explain it.

Having sex had been a mistake. But he'd known that all along, really; there was no need for it, except for the hunger in their bodies. He'd felt that stronger than anything. Needed it.

Jess had initially hired him to seduce Anne. But the plan changed. Seducing her wasn't necessary, Jess had said; Luca only needed to bring Anne to Jess, to give her a chance to... to do what, Luca still had no idea.

But he *had* slept with her. His body had gotten the better of him. Plus, Jess had told him this after he booked the hotel room. Did that make it any better? Did it make any difference at all? Or was Luca looking for excuses?

"Anne," he said, as she sat up in bed, pulling on her underwear.

She turned, hair spilling over her shoulder. "Yes?"

"I need you to have a talk with somebody."

"I don't understand."

Luca thought about what Jess had said. He'd explained that Anne would find this insane, and Jess had countered by instructing Luca to tell her he knew about all the bad stuff in her marriage. That was it: *the bad stuff.* Jess had kept it vague, but Luca thought he understood what she was hinting at.

"My friend knows something about what's going on in your marriage."

It was tragic and wrong, the way Anne grabbed the blankets, pulled them up to instinctively protect herself. It was as though she knew she'd gone too far, exposed herself too much, emotionally as much as physically.

"Explain," she said tightly.

Luca wasn't sure how he could. "I can't. You need to talk with my friend. She said she wants to help you."

"Theo," Anne whispered.

"Who's Theo?"

Anne's expression tightened. "An old friend. Somebody left him a note a few weeks ago. I wonder... So this is why we're here, Luca? Because you wanted to give me this message?"

"Yes."

"And *this*." She waved a hand at the bed. "Why go through with this then?"

Luca smiled; it felt genuine. "Because I couldn't help myself."

She returned his smile for a moment, then killed it. "You're sick. That was rape."

"What? No. *No*. We both wanted it."

"I didn't know you were going to spring this on me. It might've changed my position. Absolutely sickening."

Luca tried to explain. He raised his hands, but Anne leapt up, as though he was going to hit her. She backed away, blanket still clutched to her nakedness, shaking her head like she thought he was on the verge of an attack.

Luca reeled, shaking his head. "I'd never hurt you."

"You already have."

"I'd never *hit* you. You don't need to act like that."

"I'm not acting. You're scaring me. First we have sex, *twice*, then you tell me... Fine. Get your friend. Let's talk to him. Let's see exactly what's going on here. Because I don't know what you're talking about, this stuff in my marriage. It's..."

Her face was getting red. She let go of the blanket and waved her hand, then quickly grabbed the blanket again when it exposed one of her breasts. "It's none of your business. Or anybody's. You shouldn't be talking to me about this."

Luca was glad she wasn't throwing around the R-word again. He didn't want to think that, but doubt was twisting into his mind. He'd tricked her, sort of, or at least not given her all the relevant information. But she'd wanted it as badly as him. He hadn't forced her to do anything... had he?

He wanted to scream. He felt like an idiot.

"Did this *friend* of yours tell you to fuck me?"

"That was the original plan, but it changed. I was supposed to arrange a meeting between you two."

"Then why..." She marched over to the bed, standing over him. "You dirty little bastard. Why?"

He sat up, sensing something in her voice. She met his eye and smiled widely, then she let her blanket go, revealing her body again; she was getting kinky. What the hell? But she was; he could tell. Something strange was happening.

"You're sick," she hissed. "Tell me why. Was it *this*?"

She smoothed her hands up and down her body, looking not at all like when they'd been intimate minutes ago. There was something unhinged about the way she was moving.

"Yes," he whispered, captivated and sickened at the same time.

"You horny freak," she snapped. "Lie down. On your back."

"Uh... okay."

Luca did as she said, and then she mounted his face, sitting backward, driving down with her hips so he could taste her completely. She writhed back and forth, her hands propped on his belly, fingernails digging into his skin. She gouged harder until he could feel her cutting him, but he didn't care. He was lost in her.

"You're a dirty rapist," she snapped.

"Anne," Luca said, voice stifled by her body. "Don't say that."

"Shut up. Dirty boys like you don't get to speak."

"Anne..."

"Keep. Going."

Luca groaned and did as she said, as she kept calling him

names. She said terrible things, about him forcing himself on her, all the ways he would make her struggle. "And at the end..." She was gasping, Luca's belly stinging with the firmness of her grip. "You'll kill me, won't you? That's what you want?"

He hadn't responded to anything else she said, and he didn't to this, except to lick her faster.

At the end, she pushed her groin so hard into his face he couldn't breathe. She kept rocking like that, then she sighed – it was all such an inconvenience for her – and clambered off, picking up the blanket.

Luca leaned up, his head dizzy. "That was unexpected."

"Are you complaining?"

Luca shook his head. "I don't want you calling me that awful word anymore."

"What? Rapist?" She giggled strangely. "Don't worry. I won't tell anybody what you are."

"Anne..."

"I'm *joking*." She laughed again. "So who's this friend then? I need to find out exactly what's going on."

CHAPTER TWENTY-NINE

I study myself in the mirror, my pink mask pulled up to my nose, my matching sunglasses covering my eyes.

I've got a trendy – I hope – hat on my head, wide-brimmed so there's plenty of shadow, covering the few bare areas of my face. I'm waiting for Luca to text me, to tell me Anne's ready, but he's taking a long time.

Maybe he's having sex with her. I've known Luca wanted to do that ever since we first started. It was in his voice, in little comments he made.

She really has got the whole MILF thing going on, you know...

But that's fine. Let them have their fun. Anne deserves some relief after Theo clearly abandoned her, despite the nudge I gave him.

Finally, my phone buzzes from the sink. It's Luca.

> She's ready. I'm bringing her to you.

I text back quickly, my nerves suddenly alight.

Okay.

Then I can do nothing but walk around the motorhome. I go to the window and look out upon the industrial estate across the sparse field, the workers tiny as they walk back and forth, ignoring me for now. I'll probably have to move on soon.

I sit on the bed, squeezing onto my legs, rocking a little. Picking up one of my pre-rolled joints, I smoke it down quickly. The smoke makes me choke and cough.

Stubbing it out, I get a drink of water then replace my mask. It turns out I was sitting there, smoking, for longer than I realised.

Luca texts me as I'm adjusting my mask.

We're here.

I take another moment to compose myself, closing my eyes, remembering Maisie and all the good times. Then I push open the door and walk out to meet Anne.

Luca's parked ten or so feet away, leaning against the bonnet, smoking a cigarette. Anne climbs from the car in a big coat, making her look out of place in this weather, sort of like how I'm always out of place. Except her hair is glamorously tousled and her bare shins are smooth and attractive.

She walks a few steps over to me, her arms folded tightly, then pauses. "I take it you're the one who left a note on Theo's car?"

"I wanted to help you, Anne."

"Help... *me*?"

The emphasis stings, but she might not mean it as an insult. I hope she doesn't.

"I'd rather talk in private." I turn to Luca, raising my hand in a shooing gesture. "Luca, fuck off for a few minutes, will you?"

He stands up from the car, all bluster. It serves him right for not being able to resist Anne, even if she *is* difficult to resist. If I was inclined toward women, I'd want her. She's effortlessly stunning as she stands there in her coat, looking cross.

Luca looks like he might say something, but then shrugs and takes his tobacco from his pocket as he wanders across the concrete field: grass twisting up through the cracks.

"So?" Anne says.

"I have to explain some things. It will make you want to hate me. But you can't hate me, Anne." *Maisie.* "I only want the best for you."

"You know nothing about me," she says.

Standing up straighter, I fight the urge to turn away. "I know that your husband beats you. I saw evidence of it."

Anne's face does an odd thing, as though it deflates then returns to normal. Her eyes narrow. "What did you see?"

"I saw Patrick hit you. Well, I heard it."

Slap-slap-slap.

"I was in your garden and your windows were open. I approached the house, and I saw him walk into the kitchen and wash his hands: wash the blood off his hands, I mean."

My voice is shaking thinking about it. "And I couldn't accept how evil it was, especially when I saw he must've been beating your body. Hitting your skinny ribs so hard his knuckles bled."

Anne's eyes get wider. It's difficult to tell what she's thinking, but then I look closer. I see the agony in the twist of her lips. The pain streaked across her face. She doesn't say anything for a long time.

For a split second, I think she smiles, but it's more like a nervous tic. The same way I'd get if anybody brought up domestic violence as a topic of conversation, back in my old life.

That half smile, that almost-reveal of the truth, that every-thing-is-okay façade.

"Why were you sneaking around in my garden?" she says eventually.

I consider this seriously. I want to give her the truth. "My husband burned our house down. My daughter died. I've got no life of my own left. So I drive around and I watch other people. I've never encountered a situation like yours before."

Except when I lived one exactly like it, but this is about her.

"If I was a spiritual person," I go on, "I'd say I was destined to find you, to help you."

To save you.

Anne laughs drily. "Help me? I don't even know your name."

"I'm Jess."

"And you already know mine."

I lift my hand, thinking of shaking hers, then drop it straight away. She sees it happen. She might tell me, *Don't be silly, we can shake hands.* But she doesn't. And that's fair enough. After what I've revealed to her, she's handling it remarkably well.

"So you know the truth," she says. "It's the secret I've been guarding for far too long. Good for you. But I don't see how you can help me. This has been happening for years."

I move closer to her, ignoring the instinctive way she tries to move back. It's not her fault.

"Do you know how strange it is, hiring somebody to... to have sex with me?" Anne says. I get the sense she's speaking out of awkwardness, borne of my proximity.

"That was the original plan. Get you into bed. But it was a turn of phrase."

"Right."

"It was," I go on. "A way to shock him, I guess. I told him

earlier he could bring you straight here. I guess you've been to the hotel? I told him to cancel it."

She nods shortly.

And? I want to ask. *What was it like? Was he everything you imagined?*

"Do you regret it?"

She looks over her shoulder at Luca, a figure in the background, lingering near the road as he smokes his cigarette. "I don't think so." She turns back to me. "I get the sense you're the same, Jess, you and Luca. You see what you want and you go after it. You saw my house and you wanted all the secrets inside."

"Yes," I say, keenly conscious of how intimate her analysis goes: right to my heart, whatever's left of it.

"You learned a secret too big to ignore," Anne goes on.

"Yes." My mouth is dry. "That's exactly it."

"So what are you going to do about it?"

I look over at Luca, clear my throat, then gesture to the motorhome. "We should talk about this inside, if you don't mind."

Anne looks around like she doesn't know quite what to make of it. I suppose I should've anticipated my living situation – with my quarters covered in rolling papers, tobacco, pipes, crisp and chocolate and sweet wrappers, takeaway containers, drink bottles, and other detritus – would have some effect on her. But I honestly didn't think of it.

"I'm sorry," I say.

She smiles, because of course she does. She's bright like Maisie. Suddenly, I feel silly for ever feeling silly.

"You don't need to apologise."

The words are a soothing balm over my anxiety. I almost offer her a drag on my joint, but I see her nose wrinkling when she looks at my main rolling tray, with my grinder and everything laid out. She turns back to me, trying to hide her disgust, but I know better than to offer.

"What did you want to talk about?" she asks.

I move closer, sensing her desire to cringe back. Perhaps she sees me as a monster come to life, clawing out of the pages of a comic book, some fictitious ghoul, and that's fine; that's how she should see me right now, with what I'm about to say.

"Your life is torture. You can put up any defence mechanism you want, but I know, because I've been there. I can see it. I *did* see it, the evidence on that fat ugly pig's knuckles." My voice wavers. "I want to help you."

"Help me," she whispers. "How?"

"I want to kill Patrick for you."

CHAPTER THIRTY

ANNE

Anne stared at the woman, Jess. It was difficult to look at her, despite the mask and the glasses and the hat.

Anne had been reeling since this started, ever since Luca revealed the truth about their hotel visit.

But what Jess had said – her offer to kill Patrick – made her focus.

Kill that pathetic, snivelling, useless man. Which would give Anne a lot of money from his life insurance.

She'd toyed with the idea countless times herself; she had control over most of his finances, but there was no way for her to cash in on his life insurance herself. Police *always* looked for the spouse; she knew that from all the reading she'd done.

She'd walked into some bizarre alternate universe, but she didn't care, not when she thought about being truly rich. She had no clue what she would do, but all of Patrick's money without having to deal with the man himself?

She'd that take deal any day.

Especially since this window-watching weirdo thought she knew all the ins and outs of Anne's marriage. It was hilarious. And useful.

"Say that again," Anne whispered.

Jess leaned even closer, bringing a distasteful waft of marijuana stink with her. "I've thought about this. It's what *should* happen, when a man's beating a woman. The man should die so the woman can move on. I understand how difficult it is, leaving."

"It is," Anne said, and it was true.

She couldn't exist in the outside world, not without Patrick's help, or more specifically, his money. Alive, he was more useful; he brought in a steady pay cheque. But their life insurance policies were mouth-wateringly good. She'd made him take one out, since he was older than her, and would – hopefully – die sooner.

"But if he died one day. An accident. A mugging gone wrong. Something like that. You'd have no involvement."

"How would that work?" Anne asked.

Jess smiled; at least, Anne assumed that was the cause of the mask twitching. "Luca's really tough. He could take Patrick easily."

"He would *kill* him?"

"He probably would. I honestly believe that. For money. And maybe you could help convince him."

"I could..."

Jess shrugged. "Tell him about all the evil stuff Patrick does. Make it clear what Patrick's doing to you. What so many men do and get away with. But Patrick won't. I promise."

Jess was beginning to sob. Anne wasn't sure what to do, standing awkwardly nearby, and then the sobbing became full-blown crying and Anne felt like she had no choice. She moved forward and carefully embraced the other woman, patting her on the back. "It's okay. It's okay."

"You have to be strong." Jess distanced herself. "I get that. I was the same."

We are not the same.

"I know," Anne said. "I can see that in you. We're the same."

There was more mask twitching, then Jess said, "I knew you'd feel it too. So..."

So, do you want me to kill your husband?

"You were sent here for a reason." Anne made her voice beautifully intense. "I don't think it's a coincidence you came to my window that night."

"No," Jess murmured, sounding almost awed.

"Think about it. What are the chances?"

Quite high, considering how often he washes his hands at that sink, always that sink, almost as a petty power play like he wants the world to see.

"So low." Jess was blubbing again.

"It was destiny. Or fate. I know that sounds crazy."

"It doesn't," Jess said. "I know exactly what you mean. So you want me to help?"

"I think so," Anne said, making an effort to sound at least a little unsure. "Does Luca know about any of this?"

"Not yet. It's like I said. I was thinking maybe you could get him used to the idea."

"We can't have any connections between us though," she said. "We've already been seen together, so it's risky enough as it is. Maybe an accident would be better. Or you could poison him at a restaurant. Something so it's difficult to find out who did it."

"You've thought about this."

"Can you blame me?" Anne snapped, wondering if she'd gone too far. "I've thought a lot worse about that man too."

"We'll have to think about options. I wanted your blessing."

"You have it."

"And I *don't* blame you. I was the same, with... with Kurk."

"Kurk?" Anne pried.

Jess turned away; her hand shook, and, Anne realised, was trying to move toward her marijuana stash as though it had gained sentience. "He was my husband. He did this to me. He killed my daughter. And he killed himself. But I survived. Lucky me, right? Lucky me."

Anne had never been one for big emotional displays, but it was clear Jess was going to start crying again. And if Anne wanted her help, she couldn't afford to keep her distance, though she would've preferred that.

So she went in for another hug, ending up with her cradling Jess as she cried and clung onto Anne as though they were long lost sisters. Jess's nails started to dig into Anne's sides, the clawing was so desperate, and Anne repressed noises of pain.

Finally, the weeping stopped. Jess stepped back and looked up at Anne.

Anne's face was flooded with empathy, a painting of understanding; she made sure of it.

"I'm so sorry. I shouldn't have done that. We hardly know each other."

Don't make me do this, Anne told herself. But she sensed how significant this moment would be to Jess.

Anne reached up and slowly took off Jess's sunglasses. The other woman stood rapt, staring, as Anne removed her mask, then her hat.

Jess was terribly burned and scarred, but Anne was able to control her reaction. Anne's mother had made her watch extremely evil things in the Bad Place, and perhaps this had shaped a piece of her, adjusted her sensitivities so she was able to smile; her lips soared upward, and then she cradled Jess's face, one cheek in each hand, aiming acceptance at her.

"I *feel* like we know each other," Anne said.

It was exactly what Jess wanted to hear. That had been the trick, before Anne had saddled herself to Patrick. That was what Mother had told her. The *lessons.*

"Frida, sweet girl, you must become what a person needs you

to be. Keep sweet, and what does that mean, hmm? It means sweet to the other person's moods and personality; it means to flow, like water, around your father, your mother, and one day, your husband. Keep sweet means to know another person better than you know yourself. You do not matter. And they do."

Nadia had since abandoned these cult teachings, but it didn't rub out the useful instincts it drummed into Anne.

There was pain there, especially with the videos... *"Keep sweet, Frida, or the same may happen to you."*

But she learned more than they knew, any of them.

The moment with Jess lasted a long time, as Anne cradled her cheeks, beaming love, beaming a sense of family and connection.

Finally, Jess reached up, touching Anne's hand.

"I can do this," she said. "I can save you."

Anne smiled so, so wide. "I know you can."

CHAPTER THIRTY-ONE

ANNE

"You better drop me down the road."

Away from the CCTV. At least, Anne hoped she was right about that. She'd never paid much attention to CCTV before, but it was far quieter down this end.

She hoped Jess would see sense and use some undetectable method, but if Luca became involved, Anne wanted to limit contact. But she also felt Jess was right; Luca, if he knew nothing about their plan, wouldn't commit murder on command.

Luca nodded, his jawline tense.

Anne's feelings couldn't have been more different than when she'd climbed into the car earlier that day.

Before, she truly had wanted an adventure. And the sheer release of having sex with somebody who wasn't grotesque and pathetic. She'd taken men over the years, of course, but lately the outside had become so exhausting to her.

It was like life had nothing new to offer.

But suddenly, it did. This miracle. This twist in the tale she never could've anticipated.

She thought of the few times she'd contemplated suicide, and she was so glad she hadn't gone through with it. She could end her days wealthy and content. Perhaps find a man who was worthy of her attention.

The car came to a stop. They were sitting beneath a broken lamp post, the shattered glass twinkling from the pavement in the afternoon sunlight.

"I guess I shouldn't ask what you two were talking about."

"Lady stuff," Anne said, laughing. "Nothing *you* need to worry about, you dirty rapist."

"Anne." He looked at her sharply. "Don't say that."

He was right. She'd slipped. Silly.

Softening her features – keeping as sweet as sweet could be – she leaned over and wrapped her arms around him. She kissed him hard; he returned the pressure, making that growling noise which drove her wild. She couldn't deny there was chemistry, physical at least.

"Don't be a baby," she said softly. "I was only joking."

"It wasn't…"

"I'm sure you're right," Anne said.

"What do you mean, you're *sure* I'm right? That sounds like it's an opinion."

"Some people would say false pretences, tricking somebody into bed, blah blah blah. *I'm* not saying it," she went on, kissing the edge of his mouth tenderly. "I'm saying some people might."

"But you don't think it."

"I think you should kiss me."

Luca resisted for a second, then did as he was told. They kissed for quite a while. Anne got carried away a little, sitting on top of him, grinding against him in the car seat.

She felt so free and wild, like the old Anne was coming out, the one who'd hunted instead of feasting on a docile farm animal.

That was Patrick, a fat cow she milked for cash. She was getting her final payment.

Anybody, anywhere. Or nobody, nowhere.

She could be whatever she wanted.

She grinded against Luca quicker, digging her fingernails into his shoulders.

They were on a public street in the daytime; Anne needed to stop this. But it was quiet, the rest of the world living their predicable lives, and anyway, Anne *couldn't* stop.

It was Luca; his eyes stared, captive, his mouth twisting.

"Are you going to finish from this, Luca?"

"I..."

"You're pathetic. Do it then."

He groaned and began moving his hips. She grinned and rubbed up and down quicker. Part of her wanted to take him out and feel him naked, to sit down as he slid up inside of her, but she knew she was risking too much already.

But the way he stared at her; he couldn't look away, couldn't do anything she didn't want him to.

"You're a disgusting fucking pig." She moaned. "You're gross. You make me want to fucking *puke*."

She gave it her all, and soon he was gasping and clawing at her hips, clinging on as he finished in his pants.

She returned to the passenger seat, muttering a silent thanks they hadn't honked the horn by mistake.

"I'm sorry, Luca," she said quickly. "About talking to you like that when we... when we're intimate. I'm always so controlled. I never get to say what *I* want to."

Mum thought *keep sweet* meant give them what they needed, but sometimes it meant imagining what she needed to be and becoming that instead. A person could *keep sweet* to an ideal they created.

"I got carried away."

She averted her eyes, willing tears, but none would come.

"It's all right." He touched her shoulder softly. "I don't know all the details, but I know you've got it rough with your husband."

"Rough," she whispered, her mind spinning. *All the pieces Jess saw; that's all that exists.* "My husband beats me until his hands bleed. But places nobody can see."

Anne wanted to snatch the words back as soon as she'd said them. She remembered lying on the bed, naked, as they had sex. She remembered him kissing almost every part of her unbruised skin.

"Not all the time," she added quickly. "But he has, many times."

"He hits your body, so your torso, ribcage, everything... so hard his knuckles cut and bleed?"

Anne pushed herself against the opposite window and simulated sobbing, though still no tears would come. But her body trembled, and she made noises as though she was gasping for air; all the pain a person could feel was being felt by her, right then.

Luca massaged her shoulders, telling her it was okay.

"I'm sorry," he said.

"You don't believe me," she whimpered, being careful to keep her face turned away. She was rubbing at her cheeks; he would think she was pawing at the tears, but she wanted her face to be puffy and red.

"It's not that. It's... I'm sorry, Anne. To hit a person on the body, with all that padding, so hard their knuckles cut and bleed. I don't know. He must be doing it so hard."

"He does, he is," Anne said. "You don't *fucking* believe me, do you?"

"I'm not saying that. He must've done some serious damage."

"He's broken ribs before," Anne croaked.

Luca's voice grew sharper. *Here we go.* "What?"

"A couple of years ago, he got carried away. He calls me his personal punching bag. I have to stand there and take it. He says it's a better workout than the gym. Sometimes he makes me stand there naked as he does it, and after, when he's had his workout... well, he gets his reward." The words tumbled out, brutal in their feasibility.

"Jesus," Luca whispered.

"But I'm *so* sorry I don't happen to have bruises at this particular moment."

"I didn't mean it like that."

Her instinct was to leave or to tell him to go fuck himself, but she couldn't risk that. She turned to him finally, hoping her eyes were red and bloodshot.

Kissing him quickly – and so blinding him – she pulled him close. She laid her head on his shoulder and spoke quietly, in an almost baby-like voice. "I know you didn't. It's okay. It's so awful, finally telling your truth and having it doubted."

"I didn't mean to."

They stayed like that for a time, then Luca said, "How do you and Jess know each other anyway? I don't get it. If she knows all about your life, why did she need me to bring you to her?"

Anne leaned back, shaking her head. "I'd have to reveal personal stuff about Jess to explain that."

Luca frowned. "Fair enough. Will I be seeing you again?"

"Do you *want* to?"

"I think so," he said.

"Then maybe you will."

Unless Jess can convince you without me.

"Don't forget to clean your pants," she said, laughing as she climbed from the car.

It was still daytime, hours before Patrick got home from work. Anne went inside and poured herself a large vodka and Coke, looking out at the street through the stained satin voile, imagining a different view. Any view.

She felt like she was waking up, pushing away the constraints of her marriage, of the law, even. She was building to something truly magnificent.

She'd been lying to Jess about fate, all that nonsense, but she honestly did wonder.

Mum would immediately accept that. *Oh, something happened, there must be a cause.* But Anne had pushed away that Bad Place doctrine; she knew that, sometimes, chaos simply happened. The mark of a person was how they responded, leveraged whatever circumstances happened to occur.

Like her, with meeting Patrick, seducing him, knowing he would make a good husband. Perfect for her.

But that phase was passing.

Anne was entering a new world, one where she tamed a savage young man and plotted murder with a disfigured drug addict.

She knocked her vodka back, smiling, letting it burn, burn, burn down her throat.

CHAPTER THIRTY-TWO

PATRICK

P atrick wanted tonight to go well. He and Anne had been having a rough time of it. He knew that. And he also knew he loved her more than he could understand; he knew how she suffered, with her childhood, with all those memories, with her anxiety.

He was making her favourite, steak and chips with corn on the cob on the side. It was one of the first meals they'd shared, back when her accent had been far stronger, everything about her so sweet and perfect. It was as if she was made for him, *carved* for him, out of all the people who could possibly exist.

Anne walked into the kitchen doorway. She was wearing a baggy hoodie, making her look small, vulnerable somehow. With the sleeves pulled over her hands and her hair in a bun, she looked so cute and sleepy.

Patrick smiled tightly, hoping she liked what she saw. "Are you hungry?"

"Starving."

Patrick let out a short sigh. "Great. It won't be much longer."

She strode to the fridge, pulled it open roughly. Patrick flinched then cursed himself. She took out a can of lemonade and drank as she stared at him. He tried to smile back. She'd been behaving strangely ever since he got home. Stranger than usual, anyway. Staring at him. Smirking at everything he said, as though she had a secret joke. He wouldn't ask her what it was.

"Medium rare, like usual?"

"Wow," she said flatly. "You remembered."

She walked past him, out the door, into the living room. Patrick told himself it was okay. The evening was going as well as he could expect. Laura had rung him again earlier, asking for a *heart to heart*. She'd said she was worried about him; she was prying too much, caring too much.

Patrick and Anne were fine; they were doing better.

He'd listen to BBC Radio Four as he cooked, he decided. But then he heard a loud huff behind him.

"Do you have to listen to that so *loudly*?"

He switched off the radio.

"Jesus," she said.

Patrick didn't turn; he stared down at his hand, his terribly old and worn hand, on the knob of the radio. And he found himself thinking, *How could a child's hand be so ancient?*

"You don't have to turn it off. You're so pathetic. Do you need my permission to wipe your ass too?"

Patrick laughed. A second later, Anne did as well. She walked over and wrapped her arms around him from behind. Patrick held her wrists, probably tighter than he should have, wondering what sort of hug this was. "I'm only joking. I love you so much."

"I love you too," he said, and he meant it; his voice got croaky. "Anne, I do. I really love you."

"You're the only man I ever wanted," she whispered, rubbing herself against his back. "The only one I'll ever need. You'll always protect me, won't you? Forever and ever?"

He turned, staring down at her. There were tears in his eyes.

"Always. I'll never let anything happen to you."

She kissed him. He held her shoulders and leaned away, ending the kiss quickly, then she giggled and disappeared back into the living room.

Glancing over his shoulder, he switched on the radio, then turned the volume down so it was about equal with the sounds of the cooking. As he went on, he had to listen closely to make out the words, but the show was interesting.

It was about the archaeological finds of a dig which had found fragments of helmets supposedly belonging to Vikings. A Norse scholar talked about the reasons for them being in that particular part of England, and Patrick found himself wondering what that would be like.

Being that sort of man. A marauder, a bloodthirsty barbarian. Unchained. He thought of the *Conan* books, his favourite as a boy. But he would never be unchained.

He'd gone from obsessing over school to obsessing over work, making a few casual friends along the way, never forming any deep connections. He'd had relationships, one of which had been truly magical. Ellie. He'd been twenty-nine at the time, and she was beautiful. Funny and kind and smart and caring.

He'd looked her up on Facebook a couple of years ago. She was married, happily it seemed, with three children.

Patrick told himself he was happy for her; look, they'd *both* made it. But the truth was, as he'd stared at Ellie's husband, Patrick had wished they could swap places. He'd walk into a room and when he walked out, magically, he would be that man. But the only problem was then that man would become Patrick.

He wasn't sure anybody else would be able to take care of Anne. She might have had her moods, but she was still always so anxious, so on-edge, as though she thought her mother was going to drag her to that awful shed.

Anne had told him all about that, and it had hit Patrick right in the gut.

The steak made a harsh searing noise and Patrick jolted from his thoughts, quickly flipping it over. For God's sake.

He'd completely overdone one side, and the water was almost bubbling over for the corns.

He quickly flipped over the steaks and turned down the heat, wondering if Anne would notice if hers was slightly char-grilled. Or maybe he could scrape it off with a knife; she much preferred hers medium rare.

He remembered how they'd laughed as they discussed it, back before they were married; he remembered how she'd placed her hand on his shoulder like he was the most important person in the world.

Patrick cooked the other side, then moved the steaks to a separate plate. He sorted the corn then returned to the steaks, taking a breadknife and carefully scraping off as much of the blackness as possible.

He would make it as good as he could, as perfect for her as he was able. He wanted Anne to be happy.

If he was lucky, *he* might be happy too.

"Dinner's almost ready," he called, as he took the chips from the oven.

Some of them were blackened, so burned smoke wafted in his face. He bit down as he quickly moved the tray to the counter. He dropped it far too loudly, heard a rustle next door.

Hurriedly, he put the unburnt chips on Anne's plate and gave himself the nasty ones. His belly rumbled, but it was fine; it would be worth it.

He sorted it all out, then carried the plates – on two trays with a drink each; it was quite difficult – into the living room. The TV was on, playing a crime show, but Anne wasn't in there. Patrick winced as he leaned down to place the trays on the coffee table.

His hip gave a jolt as he stood, then he went upstairs.

He guessed she would be in the bathroom, washing, but he found her in bed, the blanket pulled right up to her neck. She lay on her side. "Can you turn the light off?" She pulled the blanket higher.

Patrick felt compelled to speak; his lip was tremoring. "Don't you want your dinner?"

She laughed humourlessly. "What a surprise. It's all about you."

"It's not. I thought..."

She pulled the blanket up further so it was almost covering her face. It was like she was trying to block him out completely. Part of him wanted to yank it away from her, but that wouldn't end in anything good.

"You went through all the effort of making dinner. So I should sit there, your pretty little obedient wife, eating it and smiling. I should *keep sweet* like Mum told me, right, Patrick? Even if my head feels like it's going to explode?"

Patrick faltered. "Do you want some painkillers?"

"We haven't got any."

"I can go down to the shop."

She huffed. "Stop making such a fuss about it."

"Shall I save your dinner for later?"

"I don't care. Can you *please* turn off the light and shut the door?"

Patrick did as she said.

Downstairs, he transferred all the food onto one plate, knowing she was unlikely to eat it. He changed the TV channel, making sure to keep the volume low, but then he thought about her headache.

He turned on subtitles and muted it, sitting there in the glow of the silent television as he ate.

CHAPTER THIRTY-THREE

"We could always go to the pub one day," Luca tells me. "If you wanted to play some darts."

I shake my head as he hands me the package. I ordered the darts online and had them delivered to his address. We're standing on a rugby field, the wind blowing, the sun recently set. The rugby posts tower over us like big ugly creatures, and I feel myself shrinking away from them.

"Why are you all the way out here?" he asks, when I don't answer.

I'm stationed outside the city. There's no need for me to return to Anne. She's a clever person. She understands what she needs to do to Luca, how she needs to convince him.

It occurred to me soon after Anne left, what I'm risking here: my freedom, my motorhome, my life on the road.

Other windows.

Plus, the weed makes it easy not to care about things which mattered more than anything only days before. It's like I'm slipping through my soul to another and back again.

But I won't leave this unfinished, so I'm being tactical.

There aren't any cameras in this random rugby field down a country road.

"I like it," I say after a long pause, tucking the darts away. "It's peaceful."

"It's bloody cold and takes a bloody long time to get here."

I shrug. "I'm pretty sure the payment I made into your bank will cover that."

"I know."

"What is it? You'd rather be with Anne?"

Luca flinches, shaking his head. "I don't know what to make of her."

"What do you mean?"

"She told me some pretty rough things about her husband the other day. Made some... I don't know–" He stuffs his joint in his mouth, takes a long suck and then blows it out slowly, closing his eyes.

"Luca?" I say, trying to mask my eagerness.

He opens his eyes. "What was I saying?"

"About Anne or something."

"Oh. Yeah, that's the thing. I'm not sure how much you know."

"I know everything," I tell him flatly.

"He beats her, she said, so hard his knuckles cut and bleed."

My whole being pulses to hear him say it, to hear the truth on his lips.

"Yes," I whisper.

Luca takes another drag, longer than the last. He's smoking heavier than he usually does. After blowing it out, his red eyes stare glassily, and he says, "You've got no idea how hard you'd have to hit a person to do that."

My flesh shivers with remembered pain. Kurk grunting, roaring, and a woman far away screaming; her voice was so distant, so disconnected to *me*, all I could think was I wish she'd stop. Wish *I'd* stop.

"You'd have to hit them *so* hard, it's borderline impossible," he goes on. "I don't understand how that could happen. I've sparred more times than I can count, and I've never seen somebody's knuckles get bloody from a rib shot. But that's what she said to me; he treats her as his personal punching bag."

Luca's words are slamming into the journalist in me, but I don't like it.

Maisie's image melts into Anne's, and my heart aches. I've been cutting down on my weed, since I need to be alert, but suddenly I reach out, taking Luca's joint.

He laughs. "All right then."

"I'm sorry." I inhale, then stop, blow it out. "Is this indica or sativa?"

"Indica. Sativa would send me into a head spin, I'm telling you, with all the shit going on."

"Yeah."

I take another drag, much longer this time, letting the tobacco and the weed fill my lungs. After a couple more, I hand it back, hoping it mellows me out. I need to think.

"There must be some mistake," I say finally. "In your logic. You sparred with men, who were probably thicker built than Anne. With muscle and fat. She's very skinny. I bet her ribs protrude. He could cut his hands on that."

"Pfft."

I snap my gaze to him. He's looking down at me, eyes glowing orange with the ember. "What's *pfft*? Use some words and some logic, Luca. Don't make stupid farm noises."

All the times I imagined telling somebody, and never quite finding the words; all those clever excuses I made.

"Have you got another?" I ask.

"Nah, not rolled."

I turn, look down the darkening field to the motorhome. "Do you want to hang out for a bit?"

"Yeah. Can do."

We walk across the field together, into the messy motorhome.

Luca looks around with none of the distaste Anne displayed, but I have tidied up a bit. Luca waits as I roll a king-skin, then we stand outside, smoking together.

"He'd have to break her ribs," he said. "She told me she ended up in the hospital. But she'd end up in the hospital *every time* if he did it that hard. So hard he cut and bruised his knuckles. I've done too much training to believe that. I'm sorry."

"So you think she's lying?"

Luca hands me the joint. Despite the quaking inside of me, I somehow manage to take it. Luca doesn't know he's causing my world to flip upside down.

"I'm not saying that," he says.

"You fucked her. Used her. Now you're calling her a liar. I don't understand what you're basing this on. You're not an expert in... in biology or whatever. You don't know about tissue, uh, density or anything like that! You're going off sparring a very select type of person."

"I'm going off common sense."

"So why did you fuck her? I told you, you could bring her right to me. Tell her what was going on in the car."

"Are you going to smoke that?"

"Are you going to answer my question?"

I stand back, inhaling, my tongue burning and the roof of my mouth dry and sticky. I can feel a strange ear-throat thing, from where I've been inhaling too much, plus the pollen out here.

"I got excited." Luca's shoulders sag. "What can I say? She

really is an attractive woman. We've got... chemistry, I guess you could call it. But it's a confusing kind. I don't know."

"So you think she's lying about being abused," I say, resisting the urge to leap at him, "but you're also attracted to her."

My head actually hurts when I imagine Luca and Anne together. It's the way his voice gets husky when he talks about her too, like it's some physical response he can't control: an animal getting ready for mating.

I imagine them together, fit smooth-skinned bodies inter-twined, beautiful as they became ruthless in their desire.

"I don't know if I'm explaining it right," Luca says.

"You saw her body." My voice gets loud, both because the idea is ugly to me and so is the implication. Silent listener, I cannot believe this, cannot accept it, and yet there are certain parts of my mind I can't ever turn off. "Completely naked."

"Yeah..."

He's got that annoying shakiness in his voice again. It's like he can barely restrain himself, thinking about Anne.

"So?" I snap. "Did you see her ribs, her belly?"

"I did, Jess."

"And?"

"You need to relax." He's moving away from me.

I've got no idea what he's talking about, but then I realise my hand is curled around a large rock; it's above my head too, as though I'm getting ready to throw it at him. Or leap at him.

I let the rock fall, shaking my head.

"What was that?" Luca says, standing cautiously away.

"I don't know."

"Don't *know*?"

"I don't remember," I shout, my sore throat getting worse.

Luca looks at me like I'm crazy. Suddenly I wish I had my mask and sunglasses and my hat. But being exposed in front of Luca, as long as we're alone, feels like the norm.

"I thought you were going to smash me over the head."

"I wouldn't do that," I say, though clearly I *did* intend that.

"You seriously don't remember?"

I swallow, not sure how to answer him. But he doesn't need one.

"That's not good, Jess. You could do anything."

"It's under control."

Luca laughs gruffly as if to say, *It clearly isn't.*

But then he lets the matter drop. Luca's like that, especially if he's been smoking a lot; things pass by and through him and he never allows it to affect him, to bury deep where it can become a problem.

Or perhaps that's a shield he uses; I wish I could know him more intimately, maybe the way Anne does, did, but that will never happen; I wish I could lie naked with him.

"Did you?" I ask. "See her?"

"Yes. There were no bruises."

"Maybe he hasn't done it recently."

"That's what she said."

"Kurk's knuckles never bled. He always aimed for places it wouldn't show... and they never bled. Not that I remember. He cut them plenty of times, but on walls, wardrobes, stuff like that. Never on me. Well, my body."

My face – my beautiful face...

"Jess, Jess."

Luca pulls me into his arms. At first, I don't believe it, but then his arms wrap tightly around me and I'm sinking into him.

He hugs me closely and strokes his hand across my scalp, making *shh* noises. I cling to him as I start to sob, and he holds me until they go away, until I'm able to step back and dab carefully at my eyes.

"I'm sorry."

"You don't have to be," he says, looking right at me.

"I wish everybody could look at me like that," I whisper, ignoring how silly the admission makes me feel. "Your uncle did me a favour, Luca."

Luca grins tightly, his eyes flickering.

"What?" I ask.

"Well..." He sighs. "I lied about my uncle. I've got one, but he isn't... he wasn't in an accident or anything. I wanted you to know I didn't care; you didn't have to feel self-conscious."

"Oh." I pause. "Then how can you look at me like that?"

Luca raises both hands to touch my face. He holds me so tenderly, it's like pleasant flames are washing over me. To be touched, held like this. I'm almost crying again.

"You're just a person. Sure, you're the weirdest one I've ever met. We're involved in some mad, weird shit. But you're still just a person."

I reach up, touch his hand. "Thank you."

We're quiet for a time, and then he says, "It's impossible, Jess."

"I saw it."

"You saw a man washing blood off his hands in a sink. That's it. Right?" He pauses. "And let's not get into that... that thing you do, sneaking around people's properties, watching them."

I flinch, trying to think if I've shared all of that with him, or how much.

Have I?

He looks closely at me: ever the mind reader. "You seriously don't remember telling me this the day after I brought her to you? We were in the motorhome; you were more stoned than I'd ever seen you, so maybe that had something to do with it. You told me about all the wonderful things you've seen. Or did you forget that too?"

His tone is almost aggressively ironic.

"I've seen how miserable she is," I snap. "How unhappy. And Patrick's cheating on her; he goes to a brothel. Anne had a boyfriend–"

"Theo?" Luca says.

"Yes."

"She mentioned him. Offhand, but it was weird. I think she thought *he* was behind this." Luca laughs in disbelief. "Whatever *this* is."

"He was an ex or something, or maybe her lover," I reply, ignoring the last bit. "But he stopped coming by. I tried to help. I almost confronted Patrick once."

"Right, so you know that Anne's seeing another man. Patrick visits a brothel. And he once washed some blood off his knuckles in a sink."

"She *told* me, Luca."

Luca's looking at me like I picked up another rock, but I haven't. "I don't know what you two discussed, exactly, but if you made her any kind of offer, then that's incentive right there. What did you tell her?"

I can't tell you. Suddenly, the idea that Luca would willingly agree to murder Patrick, based on what we have, seems ludicrous.

"Nothing. We were talking. I didn't *offer* her anything."

"I don't know what to tell you then. You're a journalist."

"I was."

"Do the facts match with her story?"

"I don't know," I say sharply. "The way you're talking, you're twisting it all up."

"And what you said about Kurk?"

The past flashes painfully through me. "Yeah, that's true. His knuckles never bled from hitting my body, fine. But Anne's skinnier than I was."

"So let's say she's telling the truth. Every few months, he

strings her up like a punching bag and beats her so badly, so brutally, his knuckles bleed to the point where he has to clean the blood off."

"Yes..."

"She'd be in hospital every few months, at least. Or she'd be dead."

"I don't know if that's true."

Luca shrugs. "Anyway, it makes no difference to me. I need to pay off the loan shark and his hounds. I delivered. It's payment time."

You're not done with this yet, I want to scream, but I manage to keep calm.

"I need one more thing," I say.

Luca groans. "Do you want these bastards to break my legs? They're getting impatient already. I've given you a day; that's more than fair."

"All right. But you have to agree to do this before I send the payment."

"I need that money."

"Then listen to me."

He shakes his head, but then says, "Go on then."

"Arrange a meeting with Anne. The three of us. We'll talk to her about this. I'm sure she's going to have very logical explanations for everything you've raised."

"I don't want anything else to do with this, with her. I'm not sure I want to see her again for... you know. Let alone this."

"Then go tell the loan shark he should get his hammer ready. Because you need some teeth removing."

Luca stares coldly at me. "Fuck me. Whatever. Fine."

I take the darts out of my pocket, looking down at them.

"Do you want to play?" Luca asks. "Because we can. *After* you send my money."

"No."

Turning, I walk into the motorhome. The photo of Patrick hangs on the far wall, pinned up. I got Luca to print it for me.

Walking over to the photo, I take it down. I'm not sure Luca is making sense.

But the thrill of using Patrick as my personal dartboard has faded.

CHAPTER THIRTY-FOUR

ANNE

Anne stood over the sink, emptying two vodka bottles. Her tongue tingled as though tempting her. She could almost taste it as it went down the drain. But she wasn't going to allow the alcohol to rule her, not when she needed to be focused.

She felt the old Anne emerging.

No more self-pity. No more falling apart when things get hard.

Her life had changed so much in the day and a half since she'd met Jess. There was a way out, the greatest scheme of all: one she'd toyed with countless times but never truly believed she could do.

She was wearing regular clothes; sober, it felt silly lounging around all day in her bathing suit. And anyway, it was good for people to see her out and about, as though hers and Patrick's marriage had taken a sudden upturn. That would also mean restraining herself in other ways, hence the vodka's sudden introduction to the drain.

A neighbour walked by, a dog at his feet. It was a terrier, by the looks of its beard. Anne had adored animals once, when she first came to England, living in shared housing with three dogs and four cats. But sometimes when she got drunk and took pills, she wasn't in control of what she did.

Maybe in her new life she would stay sober. She could get a dog then.

Anne checked her phone as she went inside. She was waiting for Luca or Jess to ring, though Jess didn't have her number; surely she'd get it through Luca. Or was it better if they didn't have each other's phone numbers?

In fact, having Luca's would be a mistake. She went to her phone, meaning to delete all their texts and call history, when her phone sprang to life.

It was *Hairdresser.*

"Hello?" she said.

Luca's tone was vague. "Anne."

She made herself as sweet as she could possibly be. "I love it when you say my name like that. I was starting to think you'd gone off me."

"It's not that," he said.

"No?" She made her voice breathy in the way men liked. "So you still like me then? Luca? You still like me?"

"I didn't ring about that."

"No?"

"Jess has asked me if you'll meet with us."

"With both of you?" Anne wondered how much Jess had told him. Surely not about the planned murder? Anne clenched the phone tighter, suddenly wishing she had a single shot of vodka to settle her down.

It wasn't right, them scheming behind her back.

Another woman might see the best in them. But Anne's defences were up. She sensed something in his tone, and she thought about the conversation she'd had with him in the car, when she said Patrick used her as a punching bag. Luca hadn't sounded convinced.

Was Jess doubting too?

"Yeah, with both of us."

Anne licked her lips. "Why?"

"We want to talk through a couple of things, that's all."

There were limited options for what he could be talking about. They had only known each other a short while. So it was either something to do with sex, which it might be; maybe Luca had been crying to Jess about the whole R-word thing, the tacit threat Anne had made.

Or it was her story; they were doubting what she'd told them.

"A couple of things," she repeated, and she started to feel more like the old Anne. *Frida*, the girl who could take anything, could do whatever it took.

She'd listen to her instincts, take the necessary steps.

"Yeah," Luca said.

"Where would we meet?"

"I don't know."

Anne knew one thing for sure: she wasn't backing down. She finally felt alive, instead of living in a waking coma.

She would prepare. It would mean going into the outside world, to several different shops, but she had a reason to. The Bad Place wouldn't hurt her, not if she had a mission; she was too strong for that.

She would invoke Frida if that's what it took. Pull up all that grit from childhood, remember all those painful lessons, and change the world to her shape.

She was tired of this life. Tired of being with Patrick. Tired of being herself.

She needed a change; she needed lots of money.

"I'll find a place," Anne said. "I'll text you. It won't be from this number. After this call, delete this number and our texts and call history."

"All right," Luca said. "Why?"

So he doesn't *know about Patrick's murder.*

That was a problem: the killer not knowing his part.

"Do it," she snapped. "Okay?"

"Fine. I'll wait for your text."

He hung up, and Anne went to the kitchen counter, grabbing a pen and a piece of paper. She wrote down Luca's number, then deleted him from her phone completely. She knew there would be records somewhere, but there was nothing outright incriminating in them; still, the knowledge that she and Luca had known each other would cause issues. She'd be more careful from then on.

Beneath his number, she wrote:

1x pay-as-you go phone

3x GoPro cameras (or similar small camera) WITH GOOD MICROPHONES

1x spray that will sting eyes (just in case: for protection)

1x hammer (just in case)

She tapped the pen against the counter, wondering if she'd left anything out.

Vodka, she wrote, then–

~~*Vodka*~~

Scout suitable location, she added.

CHAPTER THIRTY-FIVE

Luca stares at the barn. "Is she a serial killer?"

It really is in the middle of nowhere. I thought that was an expression, but here it is, this random barn in this random field. Her car (the car I've spotted a couple of times at the rear of their property, I mean, the spare they rarely use) was parked on the other side of the woods, in the car park, the same place we left Luca's.

I look at him, all tense as he drags on the joint, his hands shaking.

"Maybe you should take it easy."

He aims the middle finger of his empty hand at me, closing his eyes and inhaling deeply. He takes a monster hit; I feel my lungs burning in sympathy. Then he keeps going.

Finally, he lets it all out, grinning at me, waving his middle finger around.

"You're acting like a child."

"This is weird, Jess."

"Maybe she's worried about meeting anywhere *he* might see. Did you think of that?"

"Or maybe she wants us out here in case she turns violent."

"Scared, are you?"

"We don't know her," he says. "Not at all. Not really."

I walk away before he can start going on with his endless talking about fists and ribs and bruises and his MMA training and all that stuff. It muddles my head, makes it difficult to think of the Anne I know.

He talks too much, assaults me with words, until he thinks he's budged me.

I'm going to give Anne the benefit of the doubt.

Anne is waiting for us at a table in the middle of the barn. The whole thing has a strangely orchestrated feel. She looks fragile, her hands crossed over her middle, her hair pulled over her eyes. She looks so afraid *I* get afraid for her, and suddenly I hate Luca for all the things he said. But they still whisper to that part of me, the one interested in facts.

The undying journalist so concerned with the truth she hid the reality of her own marriage from the world until it burned her to a crisp. What a role model I am.

Luca strides ahead. "Why are we meeting here?"

Anne looks at me, like she's scared Luca's walking at her too quickly.

"Relax," I say. "Luca."

He stares at me, then at Anne. "Why?"

"Because I don't want anybody seeing me," Anne says with some dignity.

"Hmm," Luca replies.

I approach more carefully, and Luca follows until we're all stood around the table.

I get the sense she wants it between us: a barrier.

"So what did you want to talk about?" Anne says.

Luca huffs, looks at me like I'm going to answer for him. When I don't, he goes on, "I wanted to talk about what you said. About Patrick hitting you so hard his knuckles bleed."

Anne's eyes get prey-sharp. It's like she's on the verge of flee-ing. She bites her lip, lets it go. It looks odd, somebody biting their lip like that. "What about it?"

"It's impossible."

"Luca," I snap.

Luca makes his shrug somehow aggressive. "It is."

"Impossible," Anne repeats.

"I'm sorry," I say.

Luca sneers at me, turns back to Anne. "I've trained contact sports a lot, so the thing is, I know that can't be true. If he was doing that, well, you'd be in the hospital every time. And even then I'm not sure his knuckles would bleed. And that's all you saw right, Jess, his knuckles bleeding?"

"And there was a sound."

Slap-slap-slap.

"Right, who's to say what that was? A sound. Be fair, you could've been hearing anything. The TV."

"So why were his knuckles bleeding?" I say.

Anne lets out a shuddering sob, interrupting us like a judge's gavel. I turn to find her gripping the table, almost collapsing against it.

"I knew," she says, and her voice is so grave, so tragic, so heartbroken, "I never should've told anybody. I wondered why you wanted to meet, but I'm so sorry. This is too much." She brushes hair from her forehead, brave in the face of her sadness as she straightens her posture. "I have to go."

"Wait. Anne. We're sorry."

Luca's watching her closely. "Anne, but... I mean... that's not an answer, is it?"

"Luca."

"It's not," he says, glaring at me.

"How's this for an answer?" Anne screams, so shrill my ears hurt.

She wrenches her shirt up, exposing her belly.

I gasp, as pain wrenches through me, mirroring hers.

There's a big bandage across her belly, a blossom of red beneath. Anne looks at Luca, panting.

"Still not enough?" she yells, then rips off the bandage.

She stares hard at Luca. "I always used to imagine risking a little. Living a little. I always wondered what it would be like, to go out there, take a chance. And I did, with you, with both of you. You had crazy plans and fine, maybe I went along with them. But they were *your* plans. But to have this questioned, this... and I've never told *anybody*. It makes me sick."

Neither Luca nor I can speak.

We're staring transfixed at the ugly gash, the crude violence of it. Her skin is puckered red, seeping tears of crimson from where the bandage has tugged at the wound; the tears slide down her belly, and it's like her body is breaking apart, corrupting her with the agony, sinking deeply into the most private parts of her and making a home there: a place furnished with all the previous wounds, reminders aplenty to keep her convinced of the cage.

"Last night, I told Patrick I wasn't in the mood for sex. It's the first time in a long time I've done that. And it was because of *you*, Luca."

"M-me?"

"You had me feeling brave, dangerous. Adventurous. Like he couldn't hurt me. So what he did was..." She covers her face, pulling her shirt down with her other hand; she hasn't reapplied her bandage.

I move to walk around the table, to help her, and she glares at me as if she hates me, pinning me in place. I don't move.

Anne continues, "He tied me to the bed. Naked. Then he took our sharpest knife – it cost a fortune – and he dragged it across my belly, slowly, and he told me why. He told me it's because I'm a bad slut and I have to do what I'm told."

I start to shudder as her words become Kurk's, so close to the phrases he would use. I'm sure he used that *exact* phrase more than once.

"Anne," Luca says.

"Oh." She shakes her head in disgust. "I get it. I did this myself."

"I wasn't going to—"

"I severely injured myself, something I've never done before, something I doubt I have the— the what? The guts? The stupidity to do. I *couldn't* do that. You're sick."

"*I'm* sick," Luca repeats, laughing gruffly.

"Is something funny? Because do you know what's not funny? Tricking a woman into bed. Lying to her and then fucking her and only telling her *after* that you lied. That's *disgusting.*"

Luca's eyes are glimmering, like he's about to cry.

"I didn't..."

"Are you going to deny it?" Anne asks in disbelief.

"No, I did... but it's not how you're making it sound."

"Okay. Fine. Yes or no, did you tell me you had an ulterior motive for meeting with me?"

"I..."

Anne laughs, as if the world is too cruel and laughter's all she can summon. "And *I'm* the liar?"

I've become the sole member of a one-person jury, the recipient of both their expressions. Luca looks at me as if to say, *What's happening?* And Anne stares, very convincingly, as if to say, *How is he going to call me a liar when we both know what he did?*

"I didn't tell you why I wanted to meet with you," Luca says. "I didn't tell you I had a different motive. Fine, I get that."

"Your friend here hired you to make contact with me. You did. She asked you to take me to her. But instead, you kept lying to me, telling me this was a chance meeting. And then you had sex with me."

"*We* had sex. Don't say it like that."

"Like... like *what*?"

Luca waves his hands at me, but I'm starting to wonder. A very nasty feeling is moving over me. I truly like Luca, for all his faults, but this doesn't sound very good at all. I *told* him he could bring her straight to me.

"We had sex," Luca says again, firmly. "I didn't *do* anything. We did it. We both wanted it."

"I wanted it because I thought it was an exciting chance meeting with a stranger. But that wasn't the situation at all. You used me and *then* told me the truth. It doesn't exactly look good, does it?"

Luca flounders. "But you wanted it. Jesus Christ, Anne, you can't stand there and tell me you didn't want it."

"Maybe I did. But would I have wanted it if you'd told me your sole reason for this so-called chance meeting was because you were hired to bring me to your friend? I don't think I would've been in a very *fuck-me* mood then."

"Well... that's a hypothetical."

"Okay then. I can tell you, for a fact, I would *not* have wanted to have sex with you if you told me the truth. There's a word for what you did."

"Anne..."

She lowers her gaze. "At least you told the truth in the end."

"I should've told you before. But..."

"But?"

"I didn't force you to do anything."

"It depends how you define *force*, I guess." Anne sighs. "You

153

tricked me. You withheld facts so you could make me have sex with you."

Luca grits his teeth. "Stop playing mind games with me."

"I'm not. I'm talking to you."

There's a pause, Luca staring at the ground, Anne standing with her hands over her middle again.

"Your bandage," I whisper. "Anne."

"Oh, right." She kneels down, then stands with it in her hand. "It's dirty. It'll have to wait. Jess, I need to talk to you about what you did. If this..." She looks at Luca. "*Thing* we talked about..." Luca winces, annoyed at being left out. "Isn't happening, I need to know you're not going to spy on me again."

CHAPTER THIRTY-SIX

LUCA

Luca felt like he'd been ambushed. He kept having to fight away tears.

What Anne was saying... it made sense, he realised, hoping it wasn't too late. What he'd done was wrong. He *should* have told her.

Suddenly he felt like an idiot for meeting her. What did it matter, what she said? He never had to see her again.

Jess couldn't make him; she'd already paid him the rest of the money to placate the loan shark and his goons. Luca had come as a favour to Jess.

The wound looked real enough. But just because Anne had called his bluff about doing it herself, it didn't mean she hadn't; it also didn't explain the bruises.

But Luca was getting sucked in again. None of this mattered. Once Jess was done, they'd leave, and Luca would never see Anne again; if Jess wanted to see her, fine.

"I..." Jess paused.

She looked so small and vulnerable, with her big hood pulled up, her glasses on, her mask hiding her mouth. Luca wanted to wrap his arm around her; he thought of his little sister, Izzy, though Jess was older, of course.

"I didn't mean to spy," Jess said finally.

"What did you mean to do?" Anne asked, with *far* more understanding in her voice than when she'd been speaking to Luca.

Which is fair. You raped her.

Luca tried to quieten the voice. He wanted to smoke another huge joint and also to never smoke again. He wanted to be somewhere else, but he wasn't leaving Jess alone.

"Ever since I lost my daughter," Jess says, "I travel from place to place. And sometimes, yes, I sneak... I *walk* onto people's property and I watch them."

Luca cringed; it was another reminder of how bizarre his life had become since Jess had nervously approached him outside work.

Anne smiled, and for a second she was beautiful again. Luca hated that. "That must be interesting."

"It is," Jess said, her voice excited like a child's. "I've seen so many things. Arguments and sex and people taking drugs, people you'd never imagine and people you would."

"How many people's houses have you watched?"

"I'm not sure. More than a hundred, I guess. Maybe as many as two or three hundred. I honestly don't know."

"Have you ever seen anybody... naked?" Anne giggled, going from outraged to almost girlish. Luca found the abrupt change jarring, but Jess didn't seem to notice or care.

"Yes, I've seen at least a dozen people naked."

"What do you like about it so much?"

"Jess, come on..."

Anne stared at Luca. He found it difficult to meet her eyes. "Please, we're talking. You're free to wait outside."

Luca shook his head. "I'll leave when Jess is ready."

Anne could pretend she was this pretty flower, or whatever she thought Jess wanted her to be, but Luca remembered what happened after he told her the truth. How she mounted him, rode him, all that stuff she said. And in the car. There was something twisted in her.

She was manipulative, not *him*.

"Jess?" Anne said.

"I suppose I like watching other people live their lives more than I like living my own. It's interesting, standing outside their window, and they don't know I'm there so they're acting so naturally. I get to see who people really are. And I get to... sort of, become them. I guess. For a little bit."

Anne said nothing at first. Finally, she spoke, "I understand. And I don't mean this in a bad way. But if we're done here... if you think I lied about my situation, then I'm going to have to ask you to stop following me and my husband."

Jess shrunk more under the weight of the words. The world was truly upside-down, because Luca wanted to defend Jess; he wanted to tell Anne that Jess had every right to spy on who she wanted when she wanted however she wanted. Which was madness.

"I know it's wrong, watching you and your husband," Jess said.

"Oh, it was just us? Nobody else?"

"Yes, Theo. I left a note on his car." Jess fidgets. "But you know all this! I don't see the point going over it all."

"This note could've put me in a lot of danger."

"I'm sorry," Jess said. "That was the opposite of what I wanted."

"I guess this is it," Anne replied. "It's best if we all forget we ever met. Luca, if you want to believe I'm a liar, fine."

"I didn't say that," Luca muttered uncomfortably.

"Anne." Jess was making a horrible sobbing noise, like it was

157

difficult for her to speak. "I want to see you again. If we can. I don't want to end things this way."

Anne nodded. "I'd like that too. I'll need to be careful..."

Somebody's laying it on thick.

Anne glared at Luca, as though he'd said the words aloud.

"But we can text each other. And maybe arrange a meeting at some point?"

"Strange how Patrick never checks your phone," Luca said.

Anne laughed in disgust. It was a very particular and very annoying kind of laugh. "He does. I delete my texts as soon as they arrive. If you haven't noticed, my husband's a dinosaur. He doesn't know how to close tabs on his internet browser. He's an idiot."

"So leave him," Luca said.

"He'd kill me."

Luca almost snorted, but Jess had turned her sunglasses at him. He could see himself, saw how nasty and demeaning his expression looked. He stopped.

Anne suddenly walked around the table. "I'm going. Jess, text me if you want."

"I will," Jess said. "Luca, you have her number?"

"Yep."

"Use this one." Anne reached into her pocket and placed a piece of paper on the table. "Maybe see you again."

Jess watched her go, still making that awful sobbing noise. Luca moved to her automatically, pulled her into his arms. She fell against him and wrapped her arms around him, sobbing into his chest.

He held her until she stopped. When she pushed away from him, he thought he sensed some distaste, as though she resented touching him.

But perhaps that was his imagination. His dirty rapist's imagination.

He shuddered, pushing all that away. "Shall we go?"

"Sure."

"Do you want to talk about anything she said?" Luca asked.

"No. I want..." She trailed off.

Luca grinned, trying to brighten her mood. "A cheeky smoke on the way back?"

Her mask changed shape. Her nose wrinkled a little, her burnt and not-at-all-ugly nose. "You read my mind."

"I'll roll it here." Luca reached into his pocket and brought out his tin. He opened his grinder and tobacco and made a quick king-size, folding the end and tucking it behind his ear. "All right then."

They said little as they smoked and walked. He wondered if she was thinking about Anne's reasoning, the way she'd laid it all out, making him sound like the villain.

"Jess, I need to tell you something. But it's going to be awkward."

"Go on..."

"When me and Anne had sex, after I told her the truth, she didn't get scared and freak out on me. She basically... Okay, I'm sorry, all right?"

"You don't have to keep apologising."

"She basically mounted my face... And she started calling me all kinds of names as she, I don't know... rode my face? She did the same thing in the car. Or similar. Sneering at me. Calling me names as she... you know, made me finish."

Jess had stopped, staring at Luca.

"Can you take off your sunglasses?" Luca asked.

"Why?"

"I hate looking at myself."

Jess looked around, then removed them slowly. They stared into each other's eyes.

"Did she really do that *right* after you told her?"

"Yes. It's not like how she says, when she was disgusted as soon as she found out. It was weird. It was like she was getting a sick thrill from the idea."

"I don't know what to make of any of this," Jess said. "I want to sleep for a year. I don't know anymore. About anything. Let's go home."

They walked the rest of the way, mostly quiet as they smoked.

"Jess." Luca gestured to the car she'd pointed out on the way up. "That's Anne's car, right?"

"Yeah."

"I thought she left."

Luca took a step back. The weed was rushing through him and fair enough, it was making him think more frantically than he usually would. But there was something there; he dug for it.

"She recorded us," he said.

Jess shook her head, laughing in a way that said, *Jesus Christ, how stoned are you?* "She didn't record us."

"She did. That's why... oh, Jess." He hadn't spun out from smoking weed, not since he was a teenager, but he felt it; the world was crashing onto his head as his words rushed out. "That's why we were stood around that table. That's why it was all so bloody... it was like a play! Jess, the things I said back there, admitted to. I can't have that. And we *rolled the joint* right there."

"Luca." Jess had her gloved hands on his shoulders. "She did *not* record us. You're getting paranoid. You've been jittery all day. You're smoking too much. Calm down."

"Then why is her car still here? I'm telling you, think about it." His throat was getting tight. "Think about her questions. Like she was trying to get something out of us. And the cut in her stomach to distract us."

"*Luca.*"

He jolted out of his ramped-up thoughts.

"I haven't decided how I feel about her cut yet," she said. "Or any of it. So please, calm down and stop getting carried away."

"I have to check."

"Check?" Jess said. "Are you seriously going to..."

Luca jogged toward the woods.

Jess raised her voice after him. "I'll be waiting here, you paranoid freak."

He searched the barn, thinking of where they were stood and where the cameras would've been for the optimal shots.

But there was nothing, not on any beam or shelf or anywhere.

Luca pictured Anne hiding somewhere near the barn, watching he and Jess leave, then returning and gathering it all up, whatever she had, the cameras and everything. And then she could've easily hurried back to the car in a wide arc, purposefully avoiding them; Anne had no way of knowing he and Jess would hang around smoking.

She'd assume they would drive immediately home. She wouldn't guess that the weed rushing around Luca's head would make him extra vigilant, or paranoid as Jess wanted to phrase it.

When Luca returned to Jess, Anne's car was gone. Luca picked up his pace; his breathing was getting out of control. "What happened?"

"Nothing really. She walked out of the woods, waved at me, then got in her car and drove away."

"Was she carrying anything when she came out of the woods?" Luca asked.

"I don't think so."

"You don't *think* so? Was she carrying a bag or anything?"

"I don't know," Jess snapped. "Can we go home?"

"How can you not know?"

"She wasn't carrying anything." Jess's voice cracked. "You're being pathetic and stoned and paranoid, that's all there is to this. Maybe she was stressed out after our conversation and took a short walk. Maybe she was nervous about running into us and wanted to wait a while, thinking we'd already be gone... which we *would* be if you hadn't decided to go on your little run."

Luca didn't like her tone at all, but he had no choice but to believe her. Anne hadn't been carrying anything; it was all in Luca's head. He needed to stop smoking, or at least cut down.

His chest still felt like it was throttling his heart.

He was going to move on, forget about this. He'd never see Anne again. He hoped Jess was right; this was paranoia, and not the truth it felt like.

"Are you okay to drive?" Jess asked.

"I'm fine," he told her gruffly. "Let's go."

CHAPTER THIRTY-SEVEN

I lied to Luca.

I told him Anne waved at me and then left, but the truth is I don't remember what happened after she emerged from the woods.

A vague recollection comes to me: walking toward her, my hands raised, and I'm saying something.

But then it all goes black.

Consciousness returned when her car was speeding away.

My throat felt raw, as though I'd been shouting.

CHAPTER THIRTY-EIGHT

ANNE

Anne pushed the gate open, keeping a smile fixed to her face. It was evening and she *should've* felt good about what she'd done: a whole shopping trip by herself.

It had been four days since the meeting in the barn, and she was trying to figure out exactly how she was going to make this work. She had what she needed, but that business with Jess in the car park had left her uneasy.

Anne had taken a twisty route in case they crossed paths, but she hadn't expected them to hang around. She had no idea where Luca was.

Once Anne had emerged from the woods, Jess had rushed over, her gloved hands stretched outward. Anne had shouldered her rucksack, hoping Jess didn't ask what was inside, though there were countless lies she could tell.

"I'm so sorry," Jess had whined. "For everything. Oh, Anne."

It had all been too much. Jess was crying melodramatically, her whole body shaking, like she was trying to win an Oscar or something. She was a mess and, to be honest, Anne wanted nothing to do with her beyond the husband-killing assistance she could provide.

"It's fine," Anne had said awkwardly, unable to summon the necessary emotion; she felt so drained.

Then Jess had started to rant like a truly insane woman, waving her arms, unhinging before Anne's eyes. "There was The Night and after The Night every single moment and person was dark like The Night and there was pain and then endless nothing, numbness. I'm so numb. I should've died a long time ago."

Get a grip, Anne had thought, staring at Jess.

If she hadn't been worrying about Luca's reappearance, Anne might've seized on this, formed some kind of bond she could use later. But she really had to go; there was no telling when Luca might emerge, paranoid from his pathetic weed habit, spotting her rucksack and demanding to know what was inside.

"Let's talk about this later," Anne said, looking around for Luca.

Perhaps Anne had accidentally moved too quickly, or Jess had misinterpreted her meaning.

Whatever the case, Jess made a mistake; she screamed as she psychotically lurched away from Anne, as if she thought Anne was going to attack her.

It came out of nowhere, this response; it was downright bizarre.

"Jess, please calm down."

Anne walked forward. In hindsight, it was clear she should've driven away the moment Jess started to behave like this.

Jess misinterpreted Anne again, and then somehow got it into her head she needed to square up to Anne. It was the weirdest thing, the way she straightened her back, her body tremoring.

"P-please," Jess said.

And then – something happened; Anne regretted it honestly – and Jess was stumbling back, almost falling to the ground.

Anne shouldn't have pushed her, but that was it. A *push*. She didn't slap her. Punch her. Kick her. Spit at her. Anything like that.

But it left Anne with a problem; she'd counted on Jess to help her willingly. Clearly that wasn't a guarantee anymore.

As Anne was unloading the shopping from the car, her mum rang.

"Frida."

"Mamma," Anne said, thinking *keep sweet* over and over again; she would become the daughter her mother needed. There would be no "she was angry leading up to her husband's death" or anything like that. No, she was getting her life together, improving, and the death would be a tragedy that threatened to derail this new-found equilibrium; she'd allow it to, for a short time, behaving appropriately grief-stricken.

They chatted for a couple of minutes, Anne lying and saying she'd started work on the house. She hinted that she and Patrick were finally trying for a child, which was beyond a joke. She'd purposefully avoided having children with him in case she ever wanted to leave.

Inside, Patrick sat at the table looking incredibly old. He was still in his work clothes, hunched over a crossword. He offered her a self-pitying smile as she placed the shopping bags on the counter. "I could've helped with those."

"It's too late."

"Sorry."

"Why are you *apologising*?"

She turned her back to him and began sorting the shopping. She could feel his eyes on her, but she kept to her task. Her belly wound stung horribly, far worse than she thought it would have;

it was tearing off the bandage so dramatically which had done it, but that had been necessary.

Their faces.

"Anne," Patrick said, in his small voice.

Lingering at her shoulder, he reeked of sweat and his office and fear, completely unmanly and sickening. "What?"

"Do you mind if I quickly grab the oil? I'm going to start dinner."

He gestured with his hand; his knuckles were scabbing over, as they had countless times before. Anne thought about fresh cuts.

She had to be good; she stood aside, offered him the sort of smile she would have in the beginning. "Sorry. Thanks so much for making dinner. You're the best husband a woman could ask for."

His reaction was to cringe, as if he thought he'd done something wrong.

Anne left the room, knowing she had to do this: find a way to cash in on her husband's death. She needed freedom but, more than that, she needed to be rid of him.

She couldn't take his moping anymore. It was driving her insane.

CHAPTER THIRTY-NINE

LUCA

"Yeah, but I don't like science."

Izzy sat on the sofa, her Doc Martins on the coffee table, toying with one of her bracelets.

Luca clenched and unclenched his fists, part of him wanting to shout at her to stop fidgeting. Maybe it was the Anne situation stressing him out, but it had been two weeks since the meeting in the barn.

Jess kept saying he needed to smoke less; his thoughts kept dragging him into pits where all that existed was the R-word, the accusation. And the worst part was, Luca knew he'd done something wrong, misleading Anne, sleeping with her under false pretences.

He wished he could take it back. He was finding it difficult to think of himself as a good person.

"Izzy," Luca said, forcibly bringing himself into the present. "You don't know what you like. You're fifteen."

"Almost sixteen."

"You're fifteen and, let's face it, you're going through a phase. You want the whole world to fuck off. You can't be fucked with anybody's goddamn motherfucking shit anymore."

"Luca," Mum said. "Do you have to?"

Dad chuckled, eyes fixed on the TV. "That was some impressive swearing."

Luca grinned for a second. He'd always had a decent relationship with his parents; they were great in every way, good honest people. They were poor, but so were most people Luca knew. Except for Jess.

And Anne, in that big fancy house...

What if Mum and Dad and Izzy ever found out what Luca had done? What if they started calling him the R-word too?

"I'm not saying you're going to be a scientist, Izzy. That's not what bothers me about this not-revising stuff."

"What then?" Izzy snapped.

"It's *this*." He pointed at her. "This attitude. Like you think you can do whatever you want, and there won't be any consequences. But let me tell you, there *are* consequences. You know Dylan, right?"

Izzy sat up, seeming more interested; she was wearing her gossip-is-on-its-way face. "Yeah?"

"I borrowed money from one of his mate's a while back. I messed up, and then I thought he was going to kill me. He was sending people to my flat. He was ringing me non-stop."

Mum and Dad stared blankly at this; they already knew about it from a previous conversation.

Izzy gawped, then muttered after a pause, "What does that have to do with revising?"

"That's the *real world*," Luca told her. "You're learning... like, patterns. Behaviours."

"Oh, he's a scientist now," Mum declares.

Dad sighed. "Let him speak, Cait."

"It's true," Luca went on. "You're learning to quit when you can't see the point of what you're doing. That's what happened with me and the gym. I lost my purpose. I could've made that place profitable and paid off the loan. But I was weak and lazy. And that's what you're being. I know you're better than this. Revise for the bloody exam."

"You used to love science," Mum said.

"Yeah, when I was eight."

"Izzy," Luca said firmly. "You need to promise me you're going to revise."

She huffed, trying to look away, but Luca was looking at her with too much focus.

"Izzy," he repeated. "Promise me."

She rolled her eyes, then she said, "Fine, I promise."

"I'm going to check in with you, make sure you're doing it," Luca said. "Where's your textbook?"

"In my bag."

"Then go get it."

"Why don't *you* go get it?"

"All right." Luca stood. "Let's do this. I'll be your handsome helper and fetch your bag, and we'll do some revision together?"

She smiled a little. "What do you know about science?"

"Not much. A little. Mainly what I've heard in podcasts. So unless your test is about interdimensional beings or frozen asteroids, then no, probably nothing."

"What?" Dad laughed.

"He's a scientist now," Mum said.

"Okay," Izzy said. "But you're *not* handsome."

"Fair enough."

Luca walked into the hallway, looking for her bag, then paused.

There was a figure walking toward the glass of the front door. It started as a dim shadow, then grew bigger as it approached. And Luca knew, as he made out the shape of her; he knew and his gut felt like it was swallowing itself. He wanted to cry.

The doorbell rang.

"Are we expecting anybody?" Mum said.

"Not that I know," Dad replied.

"I'll get it," Luca called.

It was the only choice, unless he wanted one of them to confront Anne instead. He closed the inner door to the hallway, though that made him feel trapped.

He regretted smoking that small blunt before coming here, because he felt far too on-edge; he was trying to cut down.

Don't be Anne.

What if he was wrong?

Luca opened the door, and Anne smiled.

She was dressed like she was going to church, a cream shirt buttoned up, her hair combed back, chino trousers, a stylish handbag. Her make-up fully done. She looked so civilised and convincing and different to the feral woman who'd mounted him in the hotel room.

"Hello," she said.

"Um, hi."

"Are you going to invite me in?"

"No."

"You might want to rethink that."

"Okay. I've thought about it. Fuck off."

She tutted, so civilised. "I honestly think that's unnecessarily cruel and mean-spirited."

"What do you want?" he asked.

"To come inside."

"Like a vampire."

She tittered. "If you like."

"Seriously. This is so out of order. Showing up at my parents' house."

"Well, I couldn't exactly do this without them. And little Izzy. Such a precious girl, isn't she."

171

Luca wanted to hit the wall, but he wouldn't let Anne see him like that. Hearing Izzy's name in Anne's mouth sounded wrong; presumably Anne had been stalking his sister online. He imagined Anne scrolling down Izzy's Facebook page, grinning like the psycho she was.

Anne tutted again. He really wished she'd stop doing that. "You're behaving very strangely for a man I've got by the balls."

He tried to hide his reaction, but Anne saw it; she knew, he could tell. She understood he'd guessed about the recordings. Maybe not the details of it, but silent communication passed between them. Without voicing the specifics, they both understood; Anne had something on Luca.

By the *balls*, as she'd said.

"You're such a nasty person," Luca said. "Look at you. Look how proud you are. You're vile."

"And you're charming."

"I don't give a fuck if you're recording or if you were then. I don't give a *shit*."

"Who said anything about recording?"

Luca stepped forward. "So how have you got me by the balls then?"

"Invite me inside and we'll talk about it."

Luca laughed darkly. "You may have Jess fooled, but not me. I see right through you. I know you cut your own belly for the shock value. I know you're a liar. Knuckles bleeding against your naked belly. The fuck are your ribs made of, razor blades?"

"I'm not *fooling* anybody. You may have your strange theories about something I told you in confidence. But it doesn't automatically become fact because you keep saying it."

"We're going in circles."

"Invite me in then."

Luca stepped back, meaning to shut the door. This was getting ridiculous.

"If you slam the door in my face, I'll take what's in my bag and show it to the whole wide world."

"What's in the bag?"

But Luca knew, and Anne saw it. She smiled. "Have you ever heard of Final Cut?"

Luca swallowed. "It's video editing software, right?"

"Yes, it is. Well done. And let me tell you, it's amazing, how... how *clear* a person's true intent becomes without all those tangents and pauses and such things. *Det är ett mirakel.*"

"What's that, Icelandic?"

Anne laughed. "Swedish, my pretty boy. Do I need to remind you what you said in the barn."

"No." He'd thought about it a lot. "I remember. I guess you twisted it up."

"I have no idea what you're referring to."

"So what's in the bag?"

"Invite me inside and I'll show you."

Luca groaned. There was nothing he wanted less, and yet he knew she wasn't bluffing.

"Why can't we go to my place? My parents are here. My sister."

"Because I want you to think, Luca, really think... what would happen if I explained what you did, to your mum, to little Izzy? Maybe your dad's enough of a bald fat cunt he wouldn't care. A fat fucking ugly Englishman. But your naïve sister, all hopped up on social justice? She calls herself a feminist on Twitter, you know. It's heartening to see a young woman take such a stand."

"A child," Luca snapped. "She's fifteen. She's a child."

"I don't think—"

"Just so you know," Luca cut in. "That's what you're doing here. You're using a *child* as part of your sick game. Not a young woman."

She looked at him like she thought he was joking. "I'll explain then, to this *child*... firstly, how you tricked me. And then I'll tell your parents you sell drugs. Then I'll drop the bombshell: the rape."

"Keep your bloody voice down," Luca snapped.

Anne shrugged, then *did* lower her voice, and that made it worse; she sounded possessed. "I'll explain how I didn't give you consent."

"But you did."

Anne huffed. "Circles, Luca. And then, to top it off, I'll tell them *why* Jess sent you to get me."

"But... why did she?"

Anne tilted her head, becoming every schoolteacher who'd ever talked down to him. "You don't need to know. But *they* will. So invite me inside. And we'll talk."

"Wait here."

Luca went into the living room. "I'm sorry, Izz. It's an old mate from school. Gonna have a quick chat with her and I'll be back, all right? Is that okay, Mum?"

"Yes, of course. Who is it? Is it *Grace*?"

"No, Mum. It's not bloody Grace."

"It'll be Hazel then."

"Nope," Luca said, leaving the room and shutting the living room door. He didn't want them seeing her: didn't want any part of her nastiness, her existence, just *her* invading their lives.

He waved Anne inside. She looked way too eager as she stepped over the threshold.

He wanted her gone. Even dead: away from here forever.

"Thank you," she said. "Could I be cheeky and ask for a cup of tea?"

PART 3

"It was night, and the rain fell; and falling, it was rain, but, having fallen, it was blood."
— *Edgar Allan Poe*

CHAPTER FORTY

I t's night-time, and the rain is falling.
    And then it's daytime, and the sun is out.
It's night again.
Then day.
I'm not sure I can tell the difference anymore.

Anyway, really it's a second. A moment. I'm hazed out, staring at the ceiling of the motorhome, hazed hazed hazed out to fuck.

I remember being happy, in fleeting moments; Maisie's sandy feet shoved into trainers as we ran for the car. The rare moments of freedom. The knuckles and the *crunch* and the *slap-slap-slap* and I'm spinning, over and around, trying to find an axis.

It's difficult to remember what it's like to kiss somebody and feel pleasure.

I remember enjoying snow.

There was a book I used to read constantly, a Victorian novel, but I've forgotten the name.

I once spent an entire afternoon braiding my hair, no music

or anything, just the task and the rain against the window and my own long beautiful thick hair in my stupid naïve hands.

Hugs used to be a thing of joy, mainly in my teenage years, snuggling into my boyfriends and disappearing there. But I don't think of them as people, or that feeling as related to them. It's mostly the sensation of calm, of feeling protected, before I realised there's no such thing.

I am the watcher in the moon. I am the faceless in the dark. I am nobody. I am nothing. I am less than dirt. I do not deserve to breathe. I should kill myself. I wish I was dead. I don't have any talents. I'm ugly and unintelligent. Whenever I leave a room, everybody laughs at everything I said. I'm a joke. I was never a good mother. I deserved everything Kurk did to me. I should've died in the fire, not Maisie.

There is nothing good about me.

But there could be.

CHAPTER FORTY-ONE

ANNE

Anne sat down and gave her biggest smile to Luca.

He was sweaty, tugging at his collar as they walked through the dining room, into the conservatory and sat at the table. His chair made a *screek* noise and he winced.

Anne laid her Gucci handbag on the table. She'd indulged where she normally wouldn't. She deserved a treat after all she'd been through. Meeting Jess and Luca had been difficult, and the rest was still to come.

She had to focus.

You may have Jess fooled, but not me.

That's what Luca had said. Anne's mind was ticking over. She was making adjustments; she might still have a way to make this work.

Forcing Luca to kill Patrick, based on what she had, would've taken a lot of effort; she would need to weaponise his drug addiction, torment him, twist him.

But if Jess... what, had *forgotten* that little moment between them in the car park? Or had she forgiven her?

"Go on then." Luca gestured at the bag. "Do your trick."

He thought he was so tough, with all his fake bluster. He

was a deflated ballbag nothing. The elevator didn't reach the top of this slow-witted boy. But still, he was handsome and mildly interesting to her. She liked making him tick.

"Aren't you going to make me the cup of tea you promised?"

Luca winced. "Come *on*."

"I'm thirsty."

Luca pushed his chair back and marched into the kitchen. Anne stood, followed him, lingering in the conservatory doorway as he put the kettle on. He'd made a point of shutting the door to the hallway, looking at her like he thought it was impressive.

"Take sugar?" he asked.

Anne smiled. "No, thank you. I'm on a health kick."

"Good for you."

Anne waited as the kettle whined, then said, "So how's Jess? She seemed shaken the last time I saw her."

"She's fine. She's smoking and hanging around without a care in the bloody world. I've only seen her to drop off."

"Marijuana," Anne said distastefully, the kettle screeching louder.

"Yeah." Luca laughed gruffly. "You going to give me a speech?"

"It's an ugly drug," Anne said, thinking of *keep sweet* and the videos; and mostly she was thinking about the red eyes of the men in the videos, and the haziness of the smoke, sometimes obscuring the unmentionable things.

"Is it?" Luca laughed again.

Don't laugh at me or I'll take out your eyes with a rusty breadknife.

"It alters people's minds. It makes their defences soft, mentally speaking."

"Are you a psychologist now?"

"It's the truth. Don't get defensive because you're addicted to it."

"I'm not addicted."

"You're high now. You can't stop. Jess is the same. Her motorhome reeked of it. If you get a man high enough, he'll completely disconnect from reality."

"That's sort of the point."

"But then it lets a person do terrible, terrible things. It lets them believe what they're doing is right."

"What are we talking about here, weed or booze? Look up the stats. Last time I checked, weed has never killed anybody."

"I'm not sure that's true."

"Look it up."

I know what I've lived, dickhead.

"Whatever," she said. "Has she mentioned me? Jess?"

"I don't talk to her about it, about you. She doesn't bloody listen."

Oh, that's good.

"What else does she say?"

Luca started pouring the tea. "I'm not telling you."

"I'm done with the games. We both know I recorded the conversation in the barn. I've edited the best clips together. You come across like a person trying to defend a rape. You're free to watch it."

His hand trembled as he poured, but he didn't stop. "I *knew* you recorded us. Jess said I was paranoid."

"Not about this," Anne said. "Can I have quite a bit of milk, please?"

Luca threw the fridge door open. "What've you got in your bag, a hard drive?"

"A stick," Anne said.

"And you've got copies."

Anne laughed lightly. "Bashing my head in wouldn't solve your problem."

"I'm not going to hurt you," Luca said. "I don't do that. Hurt people."

"Rape is, some might say, hurting somebody."

"That old chestnut," Luca said, trying to pretend he didn't care, but his tremoring voice gave him away.

Anne approached him, laying her handbag on the table and leaning around to take her cup of tea. But that brought her right up against him; it was too tempting. Her head rushed with a sudden influx of power.

She grabbed his cock through his trousers, rubbing quickly, feeling him getting hard. Fucking disgusting. But it told her everything she needed to know.

She was in charge. His dick was keeping sweet for her.

"Stop," Luca whispered.

"Your little sister's in the next room," she said, rubbing him faster. "And you're getting hard like a freak. You sick rapist."

"Anne, please. Stop doing this. I don't want this."

"Fucking sick."

She rubbed him quicker and quicker, and then he grunted a pathetic thirty seconds later. She stepped away, laughing as she reached around him and took her cup of tea.

She walked over to the doorway and turned, blowing on her tea as she watched him.

He stood with his back to her, sort of trembling; she wasn't sure what he was doing. Just staring at the wall like a weirdo.

"Luca, thanks for the tea," she said.

"Yeah."

She took a sip, though it was too hot; it burned her tongue quite a bit. And it wasn't very good. "It's really hitting the spot."

"I'm glad."

"Are we going to talk now?"

Luca turned, his face tight and red. His eyes were glassy, probably from all the weed he'd been smoking. "All right."

"No, I did... but it's not how you're making it sound."

Luca stared at himself on the laptop, standing in the barn, bargaining with Anne across the table. Jess stood like a gargoyle off to the side.

"I didn't tell you I had a different motive. Fine, I get that."

Anne watched Luca, the way his face got all tight again; it was like after he'd made her the cup of tea. He was trying to act so tough, like he was the big brave man, but she could see right through him.

"Well... that's a hypothetical."

Luca watched the rest, his face a gorgeous map of discomfort. But there were only little indulgences here and there; she was mainly interested in money.

It was the purest of motives, she thought, the most practically sound. Make money, *then* figure out who she wanted to be; it was a waste of time doing it the other way around.

What if Anne simply wanted to be a woman with a lot of money who could live her life on her own terms? Wasn't that okay?

"I don't admit to anything," Luca said once the video ended.

Anne drummed her fingernails on the table. Her shirt brushed painfully against her bandage, but she suppressed the wince. "You sound like a man who assaulted me, and you're trying to talk your way out of it. See sense."

"You're evil."

"I didn't come here to be insulted."

"Talking about r... about *that*."

"Yes. That's what we're talking about. What's the problem?

183

You're being a baby about it. You're acting like a little child. Like you can't take responsibility for your mistakes. It's pathetic. It's so small of you, to behave that way. It really speaks to your character, to who you really are."

"Yeah, yeah."

"So what about rape? Since you've got such a problem with it."

He was looking at her glassy eyed again. "Yeah, I do. Anne. I do."

"Go smoke another joint, you sad pathetic stoner."

"All right. I'll leave then."

"Good. And I'll go show Izzy who her brother really is."

Luca stood, hands on hips, breathing fast. "This isn't enough to..."

"But it is," she said. "We live in a wonderful era for women's rights. There are still problems to address, of course. But women are finally able to speak out about what happened to them. And what you did to me, Luca, it would very much get you in trouble."

Luca shook his head. "I didn't do anything."

"You tricked me, and, when I discovered the truth, you attacked me and forced yourself on me."

Luca looked at the conservatory door. "I would never do that. Never. I'd die before I did that. I'd bury anybody who did that. Don't say that about me. That's not who I am."

"All very big and noble, but it's not the truth. We both know what you did."

He stared, looking like he might cry.

"The point is," she went on. "When I explain what happened, and how scared I was about meeting you, and how terrified I was that my husband would find out... and when I tell them that I was so scared, I wanted to get *something* out of you. Just something to acknowledge what had happened to me..."

Anne was flowing. Luca looked at her, mesmerised.

"Because otherwise you start to doubt yourself. You start to wonder if you're going crazy. But I'm not. You know what you did to me. I'll explain all of it, then offer this video up as proof... *I was only able to get him to admit to this, but he did so much more.*"

Luca slammed Anne's laptop shut. "What do you want? Let's get down to it. I haven't got any money."

"I don't need money," she said.

She did, of course. But not from *him.*

There was a small problem: the fact she'd been seen so many times with Luca. That would surely raise suspicion. But that was an issue for a later time. There would be plans, alibis, ways to sort it out.

She was taking this one step at a time, from quitting drinking to summoning the courage to pursue the future she deserved.

CHAPTER FORTY-TWO

Luca is sitting on the edge of the bed, his back hunched as he rolls a joint. It's like he's purposefully turned away from me. Wind blows some leaves against us, tapping past the windows.

"So you've changed your mind," I say, wishing he wouldn't smoke so much. "You believe Anne? You're not doubting anymore?"

"That's not a bad thing," he says, then licks the paper.

I study his build, his strong back, his messy hair. I'm lying maskless and glasses-less and hatless and hoodless and ready; in a different world, I wonder if I could try it on with him.

"So you don't think Anne cut herself or recorded us?"

"The recording shit was always paranoia."

"I'm happy to hear you say that."

His shoulders get tight, like he wants a massage. But I need to stop letting my mind go there.

This is more important. *Anne* is more important.

"I was so angry before, about what she said," he goes on. "About me. It was skewing things. But I met with her yesterday."

I sit up. "You did?"

"We talked. And all that stuff I said, Jess, about knuckles and shit. I was so angry with her about that horrible word she'd used against me: about how she'd behaved in the hotel room after I told her the truth. But she admitted she..."

"What?" I whisper.

"She was trying to hurt me," Luca said. "By saying that... stuff about me. She was upset because she thought I didn't want her for *her*. She apologised."

"That's awful," I say. "You lied to me. You told me you really believed she couldn't have been telling the truth. That Patrick's knuckles *couldn't* have bled. And for what? Because you wanted to turn me against her?"

Luca turns. His eyes are so full of understanding. I resist the urge to flinch beneath his attention. He hasn't been hanging around a lot lately, only dropping off my packages. "I know. I'm so sorry. That was wrong of me. I mean that."

"You lied about your uncle and you lied about this."

He frowns. For a second, I think he's going to cry.

I lean forward and touch his arm; he doesn't flinch, try to move away. "But it's all right. I get it. I'm glad I know where I stand."

"Really?" Luca says.

I smile. "I don't want to make a big deal out of it and lose you as a friend."

"You'll never lose me." Luca grins. "I'll be dropping off big fat nuggets to the retirement home."

I laugh, thinking about what he said.

It shows a new side to Anne, making up something so malicious about Luca, throwing that horrible term at him. But it also shows her character that she told the truth and admitted she was wrong.

If she and Luca are okay, it means I can finally stop flitting between the two; they are, after all, the most important people in my life, as pathetic as that is.

"I really am sorry," he says, looking right at me, into me, enveloping me in his gallant gaze. "I was trying to hurt her, through you. To lie to you, pretend I knew stuff I didn't. It was wrong. I wish I could take it back."

He reaches over, clutching my hand. I hold on tightly. He feels so firm, so *right there*.

"Smoke?" he asks, giving my hand a warm squeeze.

"Sure."

We go outside and Luca lights up. That's one of my new rules too, not smoking in the motorhome.

"So knuckles *can* bleed from... from what Anne went through?"

Luca lights and inhales and blows out a big plume. "Yeah, course. I've seen it myself during training. It's pretty brutal, but it can happen."

"Jesus," I whisper, taking the joint from him. "Poor Anne."

"Yeah," Luca says, stuffing his hands in his pockets. "Poor Anne."

I look at him, wondering about my plan, about Patrick.

Maybe this can have a happy ending after all.

CHAPTER FORTY-THREE

PATRICK

Patrick was ill, had taken time off work, so it was extremely annoying when somebody started pressing the buzzer. His first thought was a delivery for Anne. She was doing much better lately, especially with her drinking, and he was honestly so proud of her for going out...

Where's she going, though?

He pushed that question away as the harsh buzzer cut through the house again. It made his headache ten times worse. He was suffering as it was, his head splitting down the middle, his nose bunged up, summer flu or something dreadful.

Anne was out, but maybe she'd forgotten her keys. Why hadn't he thought of that before?

He jumped out of bed, ignoring the drilling sensation in his skull, and went downstairs. He pushed open the door and walked halfway up the garden path before realising he was still in his old-fashioned pyjamas, the ones Anne teased him about but thankfully tolerated. They were stripy and long.

He felt like a jackass, especially since it wasn't Anne.

It was a young man with one of those stylish military-style haircuts. He looked fit, and it made Patrick feel small.

"Can I help you?"

"I'm sorry," the man said, moving to step away.

"Do you have a package?"

"I... I'm here to see Anne."

Patrick's belly chose that moment to cramp. He fought the urge to keel over. This illness was so terrible. It wasn't just the cold.

He felt like he'd been kicked in the belly with a pointed shoe.

"Right," Patrick said.

"I'll come back another time."

To see my wife.

"You were hitting that thing like you were trying to break it," Patrick said.

"I'm sorry?"

"The doorbell. The buzzer."

"Oh."

"You must've really wanted to speak to her."

The man grimaced. He was a cocky little shit. Patrick thought of work, where he could've had this arsehole filing meaningless papers for weeks. He didn't have to confront anybody, simply send an email.

But this was the outside world, and Patrick couldn't win any kind of contest with this man.

"It doesn't matter."

"Right."

The man seemed to come to a decision. "I'm Theo. I take it you're Patrick?"

Patrick nodded. His belly was causing him significant pain.

"I'm an ex-boyfriend of Anne's," Theo said, with a certain intensity as though he expected Patrick to suddenly divine his reason for being there. When he didn't, Theo stepped right up to the gate. "We didn't exactly leave on the best terms."

"Right."

Theo huffed. "Mate, you know what I'm getting at, surely."

Mate. Patrick had never felt comfortable saying that word.

"I have no idea. Are you having an affair with my wife?"

The words just came out. He didn't raise his voice; Anne had made mistakes in the past, and Patrick had always forgiven her. She had issues, related to her childhood, and it made her act out sexually sometimes. It wasn't her fault.

"No," Theo said after a pause, in a tone of amazement. "I mean... yes, kind of. But that's not what I'm saying."

"Then I don't understand."

"All right, let me tell you this. I was with Anne while you were married to her. She didn't tell me. I only found out because I saw you both at the supermarket once. I asked her about it. You can imagine how that conversation went."

Patrick swallowed. "Can I?"

"Are you high?"

"I despise drugs."

"So you're playing dumb then. Got it," Theo said. "It took a lot for me to leave Anne. After everything that happened. I'm not sure *how* it happened, but... one second we were casual, you know. And then it's like, suddenly she has a say in every part of my life. Or, if I tried to do my own thing, the shit would start."

Patrick swallowed again.

"You know what I mean when I say the *shit*, don't you?"

Patrick thought of blood swirling down a plughole. "I'm sure I have no idea what you mean."

Theo shook his head slowly. "You're going to make me say it? I've talked a lot about this with my wife. Who I love. Anne would kick the crap out of me. Assault me. Or she'd do stuff, in the bedroom... and– And I didn't exactly want... But the thing is, you can't always make sense of it at the time. When you're in it, you're covered."

Patrick's heart was fluttering. He felt it bashing against his weak chest, his infirm body. He felt deflated. He wanted to lie down. He wondered where Anne had gone, and what would happen if she returned while he and Theo were speaking.

"Aren't you going to call me a liar?" Theo said. "Most men would. If their wife wasn't an animal."

"What do you want, Theo?"

Theo stared, as if mesmerised by the use of his name. Patrick couldn't stand to look into his eyes, so he stared at his chest instead; it was a strong, muscled chest.

"Do you play sports?" Patrick asked suddenly.

"Yeah," Theo said. "It's called running away from your psycho wife."

"Says the man trying to break the doorbell."

"That's funny. Hilarious. Are you seriously not going to even comment on what I said? About your own wife?"

Patrick stared bleakly at the younger man. "Why are you here?"

"Have you had a lobotomy? Or no, what's it called, in prison?"

"Institutionalised," Patrick said, tasting the word.

"Yeah, that's you, mate. You're so scared of her you won't bloody say a word about it."

Patrick's mind went to his childhood dog, Tricksy, a happy Jack Russell who had been addicted to fetch. Every morning, Patrick would open his eyes to see her wagging tail, or her snout in his face; or he'd feel her drop the ball onto his chest, roll down and softly touch his chin. Tricksy would lap at his cheeks, waking him up.

He often found his mind going to seemingly random places; this happened most aggressively whenever somebody made a comment about Anne, however mild... and *this* certainly wasn't mild.

It was easier to think of his life before: the one in which he'd been able to take that snippet of Tricksy, those happy moments of tail-wagging and levity, and imagine his entire life might be composed of similar joys.

There were tears in Patrick's eyes. He rubbed them away.

"It's all right," Theo said.

"I'm *ill*." Patrick sounded whiney even to himself. "All right, so you say my wife cheated on me with you. Fine. You make a whole lot of... of outlandish claims–"

"We both know that's bollocks."

"What do you *want*?"

"I came here wanting one thing, but you know what I want most now? For you to tell the truth. You were almost crying, mate. No judgement. I cried plenty after... But that's the thing. We can talk about it, if you want."

"There's nothing to talk about," Patrick said quietly. His throat was tight. There was too much pollen. He was sure that's what had done it, the bloody pollen. It was everywhere, all over the city. "If you're not going to tell me why you're here..."

"This is so sad," Theo said.

"Is it?"

"Yeah. It's pathetic. I feel terrible for you."

"Take your lies somewhere else!" Patrick suddenly roared, as a thought occurred to him: *Anne, I tried to tell him he was a liar. I tried to tell him he was wrong for saying those things wrong for thinking them wrong for putting them in my head but he wouldn't listen and I tried and I love you and I will always love you and I wish you loved me too.* All of that, in a rush, more as a jumble of feelings and impulses than words, thrown together as he threw himself against the gate. "Fuck off! Get out of here!"

Theo stepped back.

Patrick deflated. He'd hurt his hand against the metal of the gate. He was panting. He felt like he'd run several miles. He was so weak. "You're trespassing."

"Not really."

"Fucking loitering then!"

"Better call MI5."

Something annoying happened. Patrick laughed, and then Theo did, and pretty soon they were chuckling together like best pals. Patrick killed the laughter, glanced down the street.

"Can't be seen laughing with the likes of me, can you?"

"The joke wasn't that funny."

Patrick's dog had died of old age when he was a teenager. He'd been in the room with her, little Tricksy, and he'd never forget the depth of that feeling. How half of him had broken away and crumbled to pieces as he walked from the room, his hands clenched at his sides, shaking like he could kill Death to bring his dog back.

He hadn't felt something that deep in years, decades.

"What was your reason for coming here?" Patrick said. "You said it was to see Anne."

"You're not going to admit it, are you?"

Patrick stared.

"When we broke up," Theo said, sighing, "Anne stole my grandma's engagement ring. I was going to give it to my wife, but I couldn't face asking Anne. Last time we met, Anne said she'd find it; she's said the same several times. It's like a sick game, calling me so I come running. I'm done waiting. It's my ring. It's theft."

Then go to the police, Patrick thought. And then, *That can't happen.*

"Hmm," Patrick said, only because Theo seemed to want an answer.

Patrick remembered a man from work once, a scrawny junior executive by the name of Rogan. His wife had cheated on him, and he was never treated the same after that; he was always, essentially, looked down upon for it. Rarely openly – though it had happened – but mostly in the general *feeling* toward him, as though he'd somehow brought this on himself.

Patrick had quite liked Rogan, and he hoped he was doing better in Edenborough, at his new job.

"I want that ring back."

"Talk to Anne about it."

"You're fine with that, are you, me swinging by and chatting to your wife any time I want?"

"It's none of my business." Patrick then pointed at his pyjamas. "As you can see, I was sleeping before you rudely interrupted. I'm very ill."

"I'm never seeing that ring again, am I?"

"I have no idea."

"I bet she sold it the night we broke up. Or threw it away. Like the vindictive bitch she is. Have a nice life, mate. You've got no one to blame but yourself."

Theo turned and calmly walked to his car.

Patrick turned and calmly walked to his house.

Inside, he shut the door, looking down at the handle.

He imagined pulling the door open and his childhood garden being there, the front lawn. Tricksy would be lying in the grass, curled up, then her eyes would blink open and she'd come running over.

If Patrick didn't have a ball, she'd duck her head and go searching for one; she liked to stow them in different places throughout the house and garden.

Standing in the doorway, Patrick smiled; in his mind he was throwing the ball, and Tricksy was chasing it.

And then he saw his wife's face, except she was all teeth and eyes, and he felt a violent eruption in his chest. Like a bomb, except nothing ever exploded. It just kept ticking like it might.

CHAPTER FORTY-FOUR

"I was raised in a cult," Anne says. "I suppose that's what you'd call it."

I sit enraptured on the other side of the bed. The motorhome is far tidier than the last time she came, every surface shiny, air freshener hopefully masking the smell of weed.

"That's so awful," I say.

She nods. "It was. I won't go into all the details, but they did lots of bad things. I try my best to be a good person, despite what they did. I swear I do. But sometimes I get so *angry*. It makes me do things. Like lie. And I shouldn't have. I wanted to explain. I owe you that."

I lean over, thinking to touch her shoulder, then stop myself. We're not at that stage yet. I'm not sure we'll ever be.

"Patrick's a monster for what he does," I tell her.

She shudders, repressing a sob. Her pain is moving into me. "He's a good man. He was. He tries."

"He cut your belly open," I say coldly. "A good person doesn't do that."

"I don't know what to do," Anne says, turning to me, looking right at me. "What can we do? Because I don't think Luca is going to *help* us."

"Help us?"

She gets wide-eyed. Her soft face hardens, then her hard face softens.

"Oh," I say, remembering. "Yes, you're right. Luca isn't going to kill Patrick."

"So I'm stuck," she hisses. "With him cutting me, beating me. I'm stuck with that for the rest of my life."

"I want to help," I say, and she keeps staring at me; it locks me in place. The pain is coming back, the red-streaked sheets and the constant shouting and the slam of a door and the sound of Maisie sobbing in the hallway while Kurk hurts me in the bedroom. "There are refuges."

Anne shakes her head, trembling. "He'd find me."

Yes, he would. Or he might. It's not impossible.

"Can you go back to Sweden?"

"No," she says. "I don't have enough money."

"But *could* you?" I press. "If you had the money. Is there a place for you there?"

Anne pauses. I desperately want to smooth some of her messy hair from her forehead. Or to kiss her softly on the cheek. To take some of her suffering for my own.

"I've got an uncle. Stellan. He lives in Eslöv. He was never close with my mother – his sister. He wouldn't tell anybody I was with him."

"So go to him. I'll help any way I can."

Anne shudders. "I wish I could. But he's not a wealthy man. He lives in shared housing with lots of other... well, we're friends, aren't we, Jess?"

"Yes," I say at once.

"He made some mistakes in his youth, my uncle. He lives with lots of other ex-criminals in communal housing. It's male-only and they share their kitchen, bathroom and everything. So you see, I *could* go to him..."

She looks pointedly at me, and I feel like I'm missing something.

"How much would it take for him to rent an apartment over there?"

"I don't want your money," Anne says, leaping to her feet. She holds her hands up, as though expecting me to spring up after her; I watch her, wondering if I've read this completely wrong and if she's going to leave me.

"I'm sorry," I say quickly. "I didn't mean that. I wasn't suggesting that."

She turns away, her body language taut, then turns back to me. It's odd. In my mind, a curtain flutters, at the theatre; it's the pantomime, and Maisie is laughing as the actor melodramatically falls down.

"If I tell Uncle Stellan I want to leave, he'll find a way to get me to him." She wraps her arms around herself, and I imagine being her arms, cradling her, soothing her. "I hope he doesn't turn to his old ways in the meantime."

I stand slowly, not wanting to upset her anymore. "What he needs is a two-bedroom flat, with perhaps a year's rent, or two. That would give you both plenty of time to figure out your situation."

"Oh yes." Anne laughs dully. "And how am I going to magically produce this money?"

Anne's looking at me like she expects an answer, but I remember how upset she got before, when she thought I was offering her money. I don't want to offend her again.

"We'll find a way," I tell her. "I'll think of something."

"I'm not sure you can do anything. But thank you. For meeting with me. For listening to me prattle on."

"I'll always listen to you," I tell her.

She smiles, like it's the sweetest thing she's ever heard. "That means a lot. Maybe we could meet again sometime soon, if you don't mind?"

"No, I don't. I mean I want to. Yes, Anne."

She walks over to the door; it was always too much to think she'd offer me a hug, or remove my mask and stuff again, like our first meeting. I can't always expect special moments like that. "Sorry to be a pain... but could we meet somewhere closer to the city next time? It's just – I'm sorry – but I don't have a lot of money for petrol."

"Uh, oh," I stammer. "Yes. I'm... that's so rude of me. I didn't think. Yes, of course."

"Patrick only gives me a certain allowance," she says, leaving the motorhome and closing the door behind her.

CHAPTER FORTY-FIVE

LUCA

Anne was talking, but Luca was finding it difficult to listen. She was sprawled out on the bed next to him, naked, dancing her fingers across his chest and up to his chin as he stared dead-eyed at the wall.

There they were, lying in her *marital* bed, and Luca couldn't stop thinking about what had happened in the kitchen a few days previously. It was as though it had only recently caught up with him.

He wondered and hated if some sick part of him had enjoyed it. But it had. *He'd* enjoyed it, even as he hadn't wanted her to do it. He didn't understand why.

He'd never known he would want anything like that, whatever it was, kinky or whatever the fuck. But she'd done it and then *he'd* done it, right there, with his sister and his parents in the next room.

"Luca," Anne said, softly prodding him.

He turned away. "What?"

"You're not listening."

Luca stared at the door. Her husband's jacket was hanging

from it. It looked somehow sad, and Luca blinked again. "What?"

"You're being very rude for somebody who just raped my throat."

Luca didn't say anything. It was more taunting, and he'd learned not to rise to it. It was what she wanted.

"Oh, you can pout all you want, *hjärtanskär*."

"What does that mean?"

"It means you have a dead, broken heart."

"Yeah, yeah."

"So how was it?" She was toying with his chin, pulling on it to make his mouth open and close. *"It was so good, Anne. The way your tight throat felt around my massive dick. Oh my gosh, man."*

"I'm not American," Luca said, when her fake accent changed, and she laughed; he smiled, hated it. Smiled anyway.

"Why are you pouting?" she asked.

"I'm just lying here. It's just my face."

"Did you like what I said?"

He cringed, wishing she wouldn't bring it up; she'd called him all the usual names, a pervert and all the rest of it. The worst one: the one he wished she'd never say again.

"When I was riding your face?" she went on, tickling his chin. She wouldn't stop poking and prodding him. "You liked it. Otherwise you wouldn't have exploded."

"Yeah." Luca swallowed, wishing he could get away from her without wrecking his life. "I liked it."

I'm only here because of that video. He was always looking everywhere, checking for cameras, in case she was trying to get him... he'd checked the room before they'd had sex. She'd called him paranoid, but he had a *reason* to be.

"So tell me about Jess."

Luca sat back, glad to be talking about something else: glad to be *thinking* about something else. "What about her?"

"What does she think about my Uncle Stellan, for one?"

"Good old Uncle Stellan," Luca said, thinking about the fake uncle he'd invented at the start, to try and chill Jess out. A fake uncle would ruin her; there was a kind of cruel poetry in that.

"Have you spoken to her about it?"

"She says it's awful," Luca told Anne. "And she's happy you feel comfortable opening up to her."

"Does she want to help me?"

Luca ran a hand through his hair, trying to figure out how to answer without lying. "Jess doesn't know what she wants. She's mentally ill."

"Oh, really?" Anne laughed again. "I had no idea."

"She's been through a lot. She doesn't deserve this."

"What if I were to offer you twenty per cent of whatever I get?" Anne said. Sitting up, she rubbed her hand up and down his limp cock, meeting his eye, grinning in a way Luca didn't like much. "But there's a condition. You have to help me. And your first job is to tell me how much she has."

Luca touched her hips, shifted her to the side.

"Charming," Anne said as he stood, walking across the room and grabbing his boxer shorts. "You already know, don't you?"

Leave me alone. "This is wrong."

"Wrong. You know, I *fell* for that once. The idea that there was a wrong. And there is. I still believe that. But it's not as simple as you make it sound. There are shades in the blackness."

"You sound so persuasive," Luca said sarcastically.

"It's the truth," she continued as Luca pulled on his T-shirt; she wasn't getting dressed, instead lying on her side, running her hand up and down her thigh. Luca didn't, wouldn't look. "Take Jess. She most likely murdered her family."

"Fuck's sake," Luca said.

"It makes sense."

"Not if you've done the most basic thing like google her name it doesn't. There are news articles about it. Neighbours saw her running from the house, on fire. She was holding her kid in her arms."

"She *was*?"

Luca pulled on his jeans, staring coldly at Anne. It was pathetic. She was claiming to be some mastermind, but she hadn't done the easiest thing, looking Jess up online. It was sad. And yet Anne was lying there, this woman who thought she was a goddamn supermodel, like she knew everything.

"Yeah. But she remembers it differently. She thought she couldn't get into Maisie's room. I'm not sure she remembers holding her..." Luca paused, thinking of Izzy. "Holding her... when she wasn't alive."

"Her daughter's burnt corpse, you mean. Don't be such a baby. So she set the house on fire, regretted it, and tried to save the girl. She failed."

Luca slowly buckled his belt. "Sure, whatever you say."

"You think it's impossible?"

Luca wasn't in the mood for this, the way Anne talked and talked. She could keep going until Luca was so deflated he didn't care anymore. It was too much. "I came here, didn't I? Like you asked."

"Good little toyboy, aren't you? Don't pout. I'm joking. Seriously though, we're not done. Sit down."

"Anne..."

"Don't make me make you."

She couldn't do anything physical to him, but her threat always lurked. Distantly, Luca wondered if it was as bad as he thought: if there was a clean way out of this. He knew Jess was right; he was smoking too much. But it was the only way he could deal with this.

He was twenty-five, but he felt ancient.

Sitting on the edge of the bed, he tugged at his jeans. They were tight. But they made him feel oddly protected.

"Tell me how much money dear Jessica has," Anne said.

"It's... she had a good job. And she got money from her husband's life insurance. And she was pretty clever, once. I mean she still is..."

"Yes, yes."

"I found an article where she was talking about investing. It was a little thing. Maybe she put it in there herself. Maybe her boss did it as a favour. But if it's true, she was smart with her money."

"How confusing. I was under the impression she was some innocent abused flower, mistreated by her husband in every way imaginable. And yet he let her gallivant around town, *investing*."

Luca groaned. This was worst of all, when she started going on about Jess. He didn't want to listen to it; he didn't want to think of Jess as a liar or a bad person. "He wanted the money. And he probably hated her for it. She probably got it worse from him because of it. Not like you, with your husband under your thumb."

"My husband is a monster. And stop changing the subject. You know, don't you? She told you? You..." She moved closer, wrapping her arms around him from behind. "I bet you saw. Both of you there, stoned off your pathetic heads. She leaves her laptop... her phone? Her phone unlocked."

"I didn't look on purpose," Luca said. "I've seen a few times. She leaves her laptop open, yeah. But she's also shown me herself."

"Why would she show you?"

"Because she trusts me."

"Silly girl. But she has done something amazing, impressive. She's living the life she wants. On her own terms."

"That's the most disgusting thing you could say about her, honestly. She's severely traumatised. She can't go a single day without hating herself. She's never happy, not really. I don't think so. Sometimes she seems that way, but..."

Luca trailed off when Anne started to snore loudly. "I'm sorry. What were you saying?"

"So pathetic."

"Ooh, a fancy word for a drug addict rapist."

Luca breathed slowly. "Ask her yourself. She'll show you her bank account."

"It's the same result. But what? Oh, you're not the one to tell me?"

Luca stood. "I don't want any part of this."

"So you don't want your twenty per cent? Are you honestly telling me that? Twenty per cent of... what would it be?"

Luca thought. His reaction must've shown on his face, because Anne seized on it. She was always watching him too closely, as though waiting for her chance. "A lot then?"

"Yeah. A lot."

"If you tell me now, I'll let you take twenty per cent. What I want is very reasonable. A shitload of money. If you get a little too, fine. As long as I can live life on my terms."

"What are you going to do?" Luca snapped. "Find another man to torture?"

"Pathetic little boy. I'll go where I want, do what I want. I can decide that later. Money is a very noble pursuit. I want you to listen very closely. Are you listening? Nod, don't talk."

Luca opened his mouth, but Anne cut in, "If you speak, you'll get nothing."

He wanted to shout at her, but he knew how much money

Jess had. He knew that even twenty per cent of it would help him so much, help Izzy more. He'd be able to do so many things.

He could try the gym again, if he was up to it, though he'd quite like to travel. Get away. Was he too old for a gap year?

"Good." She smiled. "The next word out of your mouth is going to be a number. It's going to be the *exact* number, as well as you can remember it, from the most recent time you saw it. Do you understand?"

Luca told himself to shout at her. But he couldn't figure out what to say to put her in her place. She was so bloody confident.

"Five hundred and twenty-one thousand," he said after a pause.

Anne sprung up on the bed. "I can work with that. That is enough, yes. I will rent, of course, rent. But with what dear Patrick will gift me in the divorce... That's quite a large sum, compared to what Patrick's life insurance was going to give me, I'm sure."

"What?" Luca's skin went cold; he knew it was impossible, but he felt it. He was ice. "His... what the *fuck*, Anne?"

Anne grinned in that sick way. "Jess never told you. Oops. That's why she hired you to begin with. You were going to kill Patrick for me."

It was one of Anne's mind games. He hated her. He wished he could cave her fragile skull in with a steel toe-capped boot until there was nothing left.

"Do you think I'm an idiot?" He was shouting; he felt like he was in the kitchen, Anne rubbing him over his trousers, wishing it would stop and trying not to cry. He felt like the explosion came right from that memory, fusing with this moment somehow. "Jess would never do that."

Anne ran to the other side of the room, her arms across her middle, over her bandage. She was suddenly the shyest most defenceless woman he'd ever seen. "I recorded it," Anne said quietly. "It's on my phone. Can I get it?"

"Of course you can get your bloody phone," he said, wincing as she made a wide circuit around him, as though not wanting to get close.

I don't want to either. But she was making him feel like a bully.

Anne played the recording.

"What can we do?" Anne said. "Because I don't think Luca is going to help us."

"Help us?" Jess asked. "Oh. Yes, you're right. Luca isn't going to kill Patrick."

Luca stared at Anne's bandage. The cut had been shallow, as far as he could tell, but Jess had reacted as though she was seeing a true horror.

Anne had some kind of spell over her; Luca knew Jess's voice, knew that tone. She'd been stoned out of her head at the time. And not just on drugs. On Anne, on whatever malformed thing Jess saw in her.

"It's not her fault," he said.

"This is the whole reason she sent you to get me. She was happy to manipulate you, lie to you, use you. She's a rich enti- tled freak looking down on the rest of us. She lives a life most people would kill for, that freedom, and she wastes all her money on disgusting drugs. She doesn't deserve your pity, nor mine, because she most likely murdered her husband and her child."

"There must've been investigations, firemen and stuff–"

"You're making excuses for her. She's a lunatic who enjoys sneaking around on people's property and watching them through their windows. She admitted to doing that countless times. She's mentally deranged; you said it yourself."

"I said she was mentally—"

"Last chance. I'm done playing this game. You've made me feel threatened in my own home. Think about your answer, because I will take it very seriously. I don't want to have to remind you…"

Rapist, he imagined Izzy yelling at him, followed by Mum, Dad, Dylan, everyone.

Luca thought about Jess smiling at him the other night, smoke shimmering around her face. He sighed. "All right. I'm in."

CHAPTER FORTY-SIX

PATRICK

"I'm sorry to ask again. I really am," Laura said down the phone.

Patrick was sitting on the edge of his bed in his boxer shorts. The illness had come and gone, though he winced when he touched his belly and chest in a shower.

It's like a heeled shoe stamped on my body, many times. It's like I was screaming in a child's voice begging the shoe to stop, not believing the shoe belonged to the owner. It's like my mind will shatter one day if I don't admit the truth to somebody, at least one person.

But how could he?

He felt numb as Laura went on. "But I've got no other choice. It's this or starve."

Staring down at his feet, he thought about how ugly they were. Fish-pale, almost translucent. When was the last time they'd seen the sun? When he was a boy?

"I know we've never been close," she said.

"We were once," he muttered.

She seemed caught off guard. "When we were little."

"A little," Patrick said, wondering if that would pass as a joke.

"I didn't want any of this to happen. And I know it's my fault. I should've stayed in a marriage I *hated* for the money. I get that. I know I'm an idiot. That's what you think, anyway."

Patrick winced as he thought about the last time they'd seen each other. "Maybe what you did was brave. It took courage. I know that much."

"Well, thanks."

"I mean it." Patrick was staring at his ugly, ugly feet. "I'm not saying I agree with it. Divorce. But, well... yes, it does take a certain measure of courage to do a thing like that."

"Is there anything you want to talk about?"

Anne passed by in the hallway, humming as she wrapped a towel around her hair. She had a towel around her body too: hiding that ghastly wound.

Patrick hated to look at that. He didn't ask about it; he never wanted to talk about it. *Maybe it was Theo. Maybe you ought to fight him.* An older boy's voice, from school; he was returning often to those days lately.

"You know my answer on this."

"Do you think I like begging my own fucking brother?"

"Cursing at me? Charming."

"I hate it. I don't want to be doing this. But God, Patrick... you could *easily* help me. I looked up your salary online."

"My salary isn't public."

"I looked up the *average* salary for your job. You don't have this crazy lavish lifestyle. It's not like you're going on cruises all the time. You bought a new house, fine, but you also sold your old one. I don't..."

Anne had wanted to move: something about new scenery. She'd been getting depressed in their old place. She thought it was a dangerous area. She'd mentioned once that people were following them, and then quickly changed the subject in that way she had: the way that told Patrick to erase the misstep from his mind.

He thought of Theo, but if Theo was the follower, he'd found them anyway. *Him and his lies his truths his lies.*

Patrick snapped, "Why the *fuck* do you think you get to tell me how to spend my money?"

"Cursing," Laura whispered, sounding like she was on the verge of tears. "Charming."

"Laura..." Patrick deflated, thinking of Tricksy. Imagining her trotting into the room and grinning around a ball, tongue hanging out; it was like this was the only memory he had, the only good thing he'd ever experienced. "I'm so sorry."

"So what is it then? You hate me? We *were* close once. You were right. We didn't have it that bad as kids."

Patrick thought of the stiff-upper-lip father and the kindly mother and the everyday problems of his everyday life. "Dad could've done more to... to prepare me. Let me know what to do."

"What?" Laura huffed. "What does that have to do with anything?"

"When something out of the ordinary happens."

"Like what?"

"Just when a man knows he has to be a man, there's a way to behave... and he was limited in that way. He could've prepared me better."

"For *what*?"

"For life."

"I'm about to lose my house. We're going to be homeless. And you're whining about how Dad didn't give you any attention. When he gave you *all* the bloody attention. And none of that matters anyway!"

"I can't," Patrick said, massaging his forehead. His headache was returning. "I'm sorry."

"Because you have to be better than me. You have to lord it over me."

"It's not that–"

"And you don't care if I have to sleep under a bridge, you selfish– *Argh!*"

She hung up, and Patrick stared at his feet, until Anne appeared in the doorway drying her hair. She had changed into pink silk pyjamas, and physically she was beautiful. "Who was that?"

"Laura."

"Oh. What did she want?"

"She's going through a tough time." Patrick paused; then he dared. "I was thinking of helping her."

"Helping her... financially?"

Patrick swallowed, then finally nodded.

"Hmm," Anne said in a musing tone. "That's something to think about. Yes, definitely something to consider."

She left the room, and Patrick tracked her footsteps into the study.

He sat there and stared at his feet and he thought about his dog and suddenly Tricksy was grinning around a blood-soaked ball and it was swirling down the hole, endlessly, around and around, and the blood became the hum of the printer from the study; it called to him, like some light in a book he'd once read.

And then Anne was back, with a few printed pieces of paper in her hand. She calmly walked over to the bed and laid them with the unprinted side facing up, but he could see the images with the light shining from the ceiling.

"Maybe we could help her," Anne said. "That would be lovely."

She left the room, and Patrick studied the photos one by

one. He stared at himself in the various poses, feeling deep shame for the wretch on the page; the rest of his exposed body was as pale as his ugly feet. The beast in the photos looked pitiful, and Patrick hated him: hated him with all his soul and wanted to kill him, stamp his face into nothing, remake him.

Patrick thought of work, of male laughter, of shame.

He thought of being *that poor bloke*.

He thought of being that *stupid sap*.

He turned the photos over, one by one – remembering when they'd blacked out the curtains and Anne had held the camera – and then he lay back on the bed. He closed his eyes.

He told Laura everything, in his mind, and he told her he was sorry.

CHAPTER FORTY-SEVEN

Luca faces me where I'm sprawled out on the bed. It's a warm day and he's wearing a vest and shorts, his arms looking strong, taut, and maybe it's the weed, but I say something very silly: something I've wanted to say since I saw him outside the car rental place.

"Imagine if we had sex."

I'm laughing, but my heart is hurting in my chest.

"Where did that come from?"

"It's a joke." I reach for my joint in the ashtray, take it, smoke it. "Where were you last night anyway? It took me ages to get hold of you."

"Are we going to act like you didn't try and jump my bones?"

I inhale and blow out smoke and inhale some more. There are a thousand constellations in each atom of smoke, and a thousand more within each star inside.

I'm looking at his arms again.

"I was busy," he says, when I don't answer his question.

"With Anne?"

"Yeah, with Anne. She's going through a tough time."

214

I keep smoking. "I was so rude to her. She thought I was trying to, I don't know, bribe her affection or something."

"She knows you were coming from a good place."

Luca's voice is tight. I wonder if it's because of what I said. Surely it *has* to be that, but it was one of those stupid things people say for no particular reason. There wasn't any desire to feel like a person again, like a fleshy sensual skin-covered member of the human race.

"I can help her," I say. "You know I can. She can get to her Uncle Stellan."

"Yeah. I hope so. But you've got to be careful with that stuff."

"What do you mean?"

He reaches over and takes the joint, relighting it and taking a short puff. After a few pulls, he hands it back to me with one of his cheeky smiles. "Sending money to people you don't know. You should let me do a bit of digging."

"You think she's lying? I thought you were over that."

"It's not that," Luca says. "But there's always a chance. If it's one per cent, I wouldn't forgive myself if I didn't check."

"But how?"

"I can get more information out of Anne, for one. And if you decide you want to help her, then I can set up an escrow. That's when–"

"I know what it is," I say quietly.

It means she wouldn't get the money straight away, only when I release it.

"Maybe she could videocall you with her uncle, then you could release the rest. But these are just ideas. I don't blame you if you don't want to help her at all."

"Aren't you fucking?" I snap. "Surely you'd want me to help her."

"Yeah, we're fucking." He looks steadily at me. "Why, jealous?"

"You wish." I turn away from him, feeling myself blush. Imagining myself as a Shakespearean balcony dweller, lover beneath me. "But it's true. You should care about her."

"Because I'm sticking my dick in her?"

"So crass. Such a pig."

He chuckles, reaching over and touching my arm. "Life's not so simple, Jessica. You ought to know that."

"So you find her attractive."

Luca smiles tightly. "I guess I do. But let's stop talking about her. Carry on."

"Carry... on?"

He winces, narrowing his eyes. He's looking at me oddly, like he pities me. "You were telling me about Maisie, the park... the time she fell off the swing."

The memory's gone. Panic, panic and it hurts. I rush around inside myself, uprooting pieces of me, and then it's there, the swing going back and forth, forth and back, penduluming until it parts my lips and makes me speak.

As I tell the story, the simple beautiful story, it's like hearing it for the first time.

CHAPTER FORTY-EIGHT

ANNE

Anne was mounting Luca, reaching down between their bodies and stroking him, trying to get him excited for round two. But he just sat there, staring up at her with that annoyingly cold look. He wasn't making any effort.

With a huff, she climbed off, sitting on the edge of the bed. She heard him rustling around behind her, pulling his clothes on, the way he always did. It was so offensive, so belittling to her, as though she was some cheap fuck.

I bet it makes him feel so powerful.

"We need a way to get more money," she said, walking over to the window. It was midday, the voile catching the light; for a moment Anne felt quite peaceful.

Then Luca sighed, a proper woe-is-me sigh, and it was ruined.

"You should've thought of something better," Luca said. "There's a low ceiling with your story. Moving abroad, getting a flat... it's expensive, but not *that* expensive."

Anne turned on him, hating his smug little grin. He'd had booze on his breath when he arrived. She couldn't help but think it had been intentional; she'd mentioned not drinking to him, and this was a big breathy middle finger.

"I'd love to rake little Izzy's eyes out of her skull."

That got him going; he flew across the room, red faced, before he remembered he was Mr Zen and calmed himself down. Walking to the other side of the room, he reached into his backpack and brought out a tin pot.

"Don't roll that filth in here," she said.

He sat heavily on the stool of her vanity unit, the back of his head reflected thrice. *Thrice.* Of all English words, that was amongst the ugliest. "Or what?" His voice was shaking; it made her sick. "Or what, Anne? Are you going to stop me?"

"You're pathetic," she snapped, walking almost right up to him, but he sat there calmly, not saying anything, as he transferred the stinky plant to his metal grinder.

Anne turned away, covering her nose. "It stinks, Luca. I hate it."

Keep sweet keep sweet keep sweet... It was so pungent, maybe because the day was warm, they were inside; it was the look on his face too. A look that told her she was small and nothing, and he could do whatever he wanted.

"It's horrible."

He laughed grimly. "Why do you want to do this? I get the money part. I hate it, but I get it. But us?"

"Don't act like it's so one-sided, you loser." Anne walked over to the window, opening it wide, sucking in fresh air. "Please don't smoke in here."

Frida, beautiful little Frida, min dotter. Come here. Take the nice man's hand.

"Don't have an answer?"

She knew he wasn't recording her; he'd mocked her as she searched him, but she wasn't an idiot. Let him have his petty laughter. It didn't make any difference to her.

That was his problem, the baby; he let his emotions rule him.

"We need a plan," she said. "Maybe we can tell her Stellan owes money... maybe we can say he's in danger? Think about it. The only person who can– Luca, *no*."

She turned when she heard the *tsk* of the lighter. He lowered it slowly, leaving the ugly swollen joint unlit. "I'm not a dog."

"You can't smoke it in here. It's bad enough you rolled it. It's disgusting. It's illegal."

"Illegal," he said, with that infuriating grin. "Jesus Christ, *Frida*, that's rich."

She cringed; that had been a slip-up, asking him to use that name during sex. She should've known he'd use it against her. That was the sort of cruel person he was.

"Please don't smoke in my house. I'm asking you nicely."

"Then you need to hear something. And understand it."

When he stood, she found herself thinking how much bigger he was than Patrick. He moved with languid confidence, predatorily, like his body was one big resting muscle waiting to snap into action. "Are you listening?"

"You're so tough..."

He shook his head, stepped closer. "Are you fucking listening, Anne?"

This fear was real, and she hated it. She wanted to make it stop. But there was no escape, not with Luca, no way out.

"If you ever say anything like that about Izzy again, I don't care if you're a woman, I'll break your goddamn nose."

"Sure you will," Anne said, trying to laugh it off.

"First I'll tackle you to the floor. Then I'll weigh you down. It'll be easy because I'm trained and you're tiny. Then I'll hold the back of your head with one hand. With my other, I'll hit you once, hard, right on the end of the nose. Do you think that would be difficult for me?"

The cut on her belly felt like it was burning. This was unacceptable, threatening, sexist, *evil* the way he was speaking to her: using his size and his sheer bulk to make her feel like her wishes didn't matter. But he wasn't coming to his senses; he was stubborn, as he stepped closer, staring down, right into her eyes.

"Really think about it," he went on, boozy breath assailing her. "If there were no laws, no standards, and I wanted to hurt you. Really think about how simple it would be for me. There would be nothing you could do."

"You'd have to kill me," she said, finally finding her voice. "And how would it look, I wonder? When that video surfaces? And I show up with a bruised nose?"

He faltered, wincing as if she'd struck him. *The pen is mightier than the sword.* This idiot had probably never heard that phrase; or, if he had, he had no clue what it meant.

But then he hardened again, shrugging. "Then fine. That's how it is. If you ever say anything about my sister again, I'll kill you. Let's go with that."

"You're not some tough guy." Anne hated the tremor in her voice. "Go outside if you want to smoke that shit."

"Say something about Izzy." He was smiling strangely. "Go on. You love your little jokes. You're so funny."

"Outside," she snapped. "I'm telling you to get *out* of my house."

"Fine by me."

He walked to the door quickly, and she could tell he wanted to hit something. *I can break objects. Look how impressive I am.* It took a seriously sick and immature individual to think something like that, let alone say it.

Anne followed him out to the hall. "Just to smoke that," she told him. "We still need to decide on a firm plan."

"I'm going home."

"Wait!"

Luca paused halfway down the stairs, glaring up at her. "Seriously, I'm not your pet. Stop shouting at me like that."

"We have to decide–"

"You already said. Tell her good old Uncle Stellan owes money."

"Will she believe it?"

Luca stared for far too long; his eyes were horribly glassy again. "She'll believe anything you tell her."

Anne felt a nice sizzle move over her body, and she wanted to somehow make him stay. But it was important, with men, to be able to judge when they were too lost in their macho feelings. Luca was over the edge; she'd force him to breaking point if she pushed too hard.

"Are you getting her nice and high?" Anne asked.

Luca looked down. "Yeah, I am. She's going to believe everything."

"And you get your money. More than a little rat like you ever could've dreamed."

"Yeah," Luca said, turning away as he lit his joint. "As long as you keep my sister's name out of your mouth."

He left the house and slammed the door.

She wanted to run down the stairs, throw the door open, shout something that would hurt him. But she was smarter than him. Her throat did an annoying itching thing, as if telling her to make a vodka and Coke, a cold one, with plenty of ice, and a straw, and maybe a lime wedge.

She was really, really going to enjoy her first drink, when she was in Eslöv with her good old Uncle Stellan.

CHAPTER FORTY-NINE

I'm so tired, melting into the bed, the fire of my brain causing the wax to drip-drip-drip onto the sheets. The ceiling is not there, not a little bit. I'm staring and trying to make sense of it, as pieces of me fall away, soaking the sheets and solidifying suddenly, fusing me more securely to the mattress.

"It's awful," Luca says, and I remember he's here, that I'm not melting; I'm lying in bed. "I googled them. The loan sharks. Stellan's in a bad spot. They're real nasty bastards... the sharks, I mean, not Anne's uncle."

"Yeah," Jess said, and Luca passed her something; it was a joint.

She watched her hand take it and then she was inhaling, and she could feel every single particle of smoke flowing into her body, becoming her, until she slipped ethereally through her skin and went to the not-there ceiling.

Gazing down at the shrunken figure on the bed, the pitiful little wasted-looking thing, she felt smoke in her lungs and she breathed in some more.

The blood falls,
And the wedding calls,

But there's pain in the vow,
Won't the sadist take a bow...

She– I– me... I'm sitting up, rubbing my face.

"Jess, you're getting ash everywhere."

I'm not sure what he's talking about. Water's flowing down my throat, and I'm holding the glass. I gasp, clutch the glass, and think of grass, sun-shaded and verdant and beautifully bountiful.

"What are you smiling about?"

"Grass."

Luca chuckles. "Right. How stoned are you?"

"On a scale... It's heavy."

"Jesus."

"Christ... cripes, gripes, mics, as in phones. Home, zone, loan. *Loan.*" I giggle, like a little girl, like a carefree kid, and I finally understand what it means to be high, truly high.

"Loan," Luca says. "Funny."

"But it's not a loan," I say, remembering... *ish.*

A wish for your dish? That was Maisie, wearing her angel wings, a magic wand in her hand and the light of naivety in her eyes. She truly believed, the perfect girl, she could grant a wish. And she'd been so proud of the rhyme.

Then the door opened, Kurk walked in.

I didn't think you'd be home this early...

I've got some bad news...

He'd lost his job, which was my fault. Always my fault.

I wish I could slip back into *that* skin, into the woman who had everything a person could reasonably ever want. She had unburned flesh and a working body and the luxury of never provoking disgust on a stranger's face; most of all, she had Maisie, a girl whose brightness was so rarely dimmed by the things she heard, saw.

I'd leap up from the table like a feral animal, a knife in my hand.

I'd stab him quickly, while he was shocked, in that brief moment before he thought to overpower me. Then I'd stab him again, again, and no matter what, I'd keep going.

If Maisie cried and screamed, even if he was already dead, I wouldn't stop. I'd have to be sure. If I hurt him badly and he woke...

No; that would be too much–

"Jess?"

I swallow; my throat is dry. "Yeah."

"It's bad, isn't it?"

"Yes, it's bad. Who are they again?"

Luca sounds as if he's getting bored with my unreliable memory. "I told you. One of the blokes, he's this well-known gangster up there. He was in the newspaper for racketeering, robbery, loads of stuff. He's out now, and he's collecting on old debts. Apparently Stellan borrowed from him in prison."

"Right," I say. "So Anne can't leave to be with him."

"They'll kill him if he doesn't pay."

"Oh."

My brain is a series of rivers, pitted out into the earth of my matter. Some are deeper and are some are shallower, and they cross over each other, but they are all flowing, gushing through me, innumerable times in the tiniest portion of a moment. I can feel some of them clashing, the larger rivers cutting into smaller ones, the water splashing everywhere, drenching the surrounding terrain.

"Jess."

"Yeah."

"It's a lot," Luca said. "He owes a lot, I mean."

"All right."

The Night is raging, flickering to life in each droplet of the collision. The water hisses like fire and Maisie's face shimmers across it all; Kurk is there, and Maisie's screaming becomes the sound of the waves. And then the waves crash into silence.

She did scream; she didn't. I found her, carried her; she burnt to ash in her room alone.

Nothing ever stands still long enough for me to know.

"Do you want to know how much?" Luca asks.

My eyes are closed. I'm not sure when I did that, but I'm wondering if that's the reason for Luca's taut tone.

"Yes."

"Five hundred thousand."

That seems like an awfully high number. Jess smiled; *I* smile. I am smiling, because the voice in my head sounds like a young determined journalist, with some, well, *sassiness* in her voice. She sounds like a I-won't-take-your-shit woman.

"That's insane," I say.

"I know. But if he can't pay them, he's a dead man. And then Anne has nowhere to go."

"You sound like you love her."

I open my eyes, look over at him.

"Oh yeah," he says sarcastically. "I can't get enough of her."

"You talk about her a lot."

"It's kind of time sensitive. That's all. I thought you wanted to help her."

Of course I did; I do. It's not that. He doesn't understand. I feel like nobody does, and me least of all. But that's not the point.

The point is— It's his voice, the emotion in it when he says her name. I don't like it. I'm allowed to not like something, aren't I? Not everything has to be complicated.

"Yeah."

"Do you still want to help her?"

"Yes."

"Then why all the jealousy?" Luca grins, trying to be cheeky and attractive, to make this moment something it isn't. "Is this because I turned you down?"

I avert my gaze. It's such a true thing, silent listener, that statement; the gaze is a projective, and I am averting its course. But perhaps deflect would be better; he bounces it back at me, and the momentum causes my head to turn.

"I don't remember that."

"Because if you're feeling stressed..."

I turn to him quickly, my everything tremoring quite badly, angrily, as I sit up in bed and feel the swirling mess in my head trying to send me back. "That's such a sick thing to say."

"How?" Luca looks at me like he's actually confused, which makes it worse.

"So you're saying you could make love to me?" I snap. "If it came right down to it. You think we *could*... those days are behind me. I can never be a person again."

Luca shuffles down the bed, shaking his head slowly. "You *are* a person, Jess."

"Don't say stuff like that. It's not realistic."

"But you *can*, right..."

"Yes," I snap, my heart picking up a little quicker, as I warn it not to. "Obviously. I'm not dead."

"Right." Luca grins, laughing. "Maybe we should schedule a date."

"Ha, ha," I say. "You're a comedian."

"We could." He looks like he's thinking about something. "If you really wanted to. I mean... what are we saying. *Do* you want to?"

I'm still trying to figure out if this is a joke. My body is telling me I want to, and I think of Korey's laugh in the background of our early phone conversations, then another woman's, and another.

But then it's me, my voice, and he's smiling, like he means it. My face is uncovered and I'm smiling too.

"I'd like..." I'm fumbling. "I'd be interested– Because, well, I've never... not since, before, and that was..."

I shake my head, knowing it was stupid to think I could get all these words out.

But then Luca reaches over, softly touching my chin, so gently, and I feel his warmth moving up and down my body. Is he going to kiss me now?

But there's that calculating look in his eyes, and I know he needs to wait. I can guess why. But I won't think about that: any chemical assistance he happens to require. Maybe that's not the reason; maybe I'm being mean.

Push that part away; focus on the poetry, the closeness. Is this weird?

I touch his hand, and I decide I don't care if it's strange. I don't care if it will make things awkward.

I want this, to feel somebody's body close to mine, *Luca's* body...

"But," I say.

He withdraws his hand.

"You have to be very..."

"I'll be gentle," he says, reading me, the only one who can. "And I'll stop the second you tell me to."

I swallow, my eyes stinging. "It's fine if this is a joke."

"It's not a joke."

"But it's fine if it is."

CHAPTER FIFTY

LUCA

Come to me, boy.

L uca heard the text in his head as he closed the gate behind him and approached the big ugly house.

Anne said it was part of their dirty talking, that they both enjoyed it; clearly, he did, or he wouldn't come. She only ever mentioned the blackmail video if he pressed her on it. And only then in a dismissive, roundabout way. She was so clever, Anne, *clever clever clever Anne.*

His footsteps took him from the path; he stumbled back onto it. He'd met up with an old mate, who didn't smoke anymore, so they'd had a few pints at the pub; that had made him want more, then the text had come. He had seven ciders in his backpack.

Anne was waiting at the door, standing in the late-afternoon sun in a nightgown, her leg arched. She'd shaved her legs, done her hair, make-up, the whole deal.

Luca felt sick; the cider was bubbling up his throat. He swallowed it down.

"What's the matter with you?" she asked.

I don't drink, she'd bragged a couple of nights ago. *I'm teetotal. You're the pathetic drug addict.*

Luca was interested to see what she'd be like after a couple of drinks. How thin was this mask she was wearing? If a person became a complete dickhead after one or two pints, the chances of them *being* a dickhead were much higher. Blackout was a different story, maybe; was a person truly themselves if they weren't there at the time? But their body was–

"Luca?"

She walked down the steps, doing her concerned routine.

"I'm fine." He moved back, around her, and then approached the house. "You're so bloody dramatic."

"And you're so charming."

He walked into the house and straight into the kitchen. Anne followed closely behind. When he laid his bag down and started loading the ciders into the fridge, he kept watch on her. He saw the flicker there, the annoyance, but then she visibly hid it.

"So you're an alcoholic now then?"

"Nothing wrong with a few drinks on a sunny day," Luca said. "You're welcome to one if you want."

She waved a hand, made a civilised *tsk* noise. He really heard the Swedish in her when she did that. If she wasn't who she was, it would be lovely. Cute. "I don't drink, and definitely not *that*."

"Well, if you change your mind..."

Luca opened one, and the *tsk* was similar to the noise she had made. He drank down a good half of it, hating the taste a little. It was cider and blackcurrant, but still, he wasn't much of a drinker. But the effects were good; they worked.

He felt like suddenly he didn't give a single fuck, and he drank some more.

"Such a pig," she said.

"I'm fine with taking my ciders on the road, lady."

She winced; she didn't like that nickname. It made her feel old. Like a perverted grotesque thing doing what she wanted because nobody ever stopped her. "We're almost at the end, and you're acting like an infant."

"I'm sorry, lady."

She winced again. Luca sipped more cider, then took another from the fridge and carried both toward the hallway. "Let's get this over with then."

She was huffing and puffing, but Luca was already stomping up the stairs. He drank as he walked, taking the steps three at a time, slamming his feet. He finished his cider and crumpled the can, dropping it onto the carpet; purple beads sank into the cream as he passed.

"So tough," Anne was saying, blah-blah-blah was all she ever did. "Such a big strong bear, aren't you? Pathetic. You think you're scaring me?"

Luca turned, opened his second cider, and stared her right in the face. He felt something in him trying to make him look away. She was sneering, then he kept staring, and her expression changed a little. She looked almost human.

"What– are you going to hit me?"

Luca laughed. "I'd never hit a woman."

"Just rape one."

His hand trembled as he took another sip, then he grinned. "I love that one. It's your funniest joke."

She climbed onto the bed, did that wannabe sexy knee-walking thing, letting her gown fall to her shoulders and expose her bra. Luca stared, sipped; he really wasn't interested.

"I'm probably too drunk," he told her, taking another sip. "I won't be any good to you."

She shook her head slowly, moaning in that way he liked, or at least part of him did. Maybe it was more accurate to say that it activated certain parts of him; that was all. What he wanted or liked didn't come into it.

She went to the end of the bed, lay back, opened her legs and started stroking over her underwear.

Luca stood still, sipped, thought of chairs: four-legged chairs, and stools, and computer ones with ergonomic back support. He thought of a kite he'd seen once as a kid. He remembered the smell of his failed gym.

"You're not *trying* to be in the mood." She sat up. "What do you want? Do you want to feel like a man?"

"I want to go home."

She giggled, shaking her head as she stood. Walking over to him, she brought a heady scent of perfume. And there was *her* smell, the mammal in him responding, making him nothing more than a dog to stud out.

She rubbed the outside of his trousers. "You don't want to go home."

He tried to keep thinking of the chairs and everything, the kites and stuff, but her hand felt... it wasn't *good*. That wasn't it.

She was fit, he told himself: a fit older bird. But he didn't feel that way. He wasn't sure what to do, or how he felt, as she kept going. His body was responding, despite the booze and the weed. She was moaning all breathily.

"That's it," she whispered. "You're getting solid for me. Aren't you?"

"Yes," he said, taking another sip.

She huffed; he felt her glaring at him. "You're rock hard, baby."

"Yeah."

She moved away. "I've been looking forward to seeing you all day. But it's like you're not here with me, and you're definitely not trying. It's not fair to treat me this way. Look at how much effort *I* put in... you're treating me like I don't matter!"

Luca took a sip of his cider.

Anne opened and closed her hands, twitchy, like she wanted to hurt something. But she couldn't hurt him; he wasn't going to fall for her manipulation tactics, the waterworks, the melodramatic crap.

"What do you want?" she asked, all breathy again. *Like a switch.* "Anything to get that pout off your face."

"Anything?"

She stared a challenge in his eyes. "Y-yes."

The hesitation tickled some nasty part of Luca. He didn't like it, and he knew he'd be able to stop if the booze wasn't rushing around his body. Or maybe that was an excuse.

He stepped closer, staring down into her face which, suddenly, seemed somehow vulnerable. "Get on your knees."

She made to laugh; except for their first time, she'd always been in charge. But then she seemed to come to a decision. "If it'll stop your whining."

She knelt beneath him. Luca placed his drink on the bedside table, then returned to her, unbuttoning his jeans and pulling them down around his knees. He pulled his boxers down and took his cock in his hand, stepping forward as he cradled the back of Anne's head.

"Open your mouth," he told her.

She stared up at him, bracing her hands on his thighs, digging her fingernails into him. "Is this it, Luca? Is this what makes you feel like a man?"

"Open your mouth," he said again.

She made a moaning noise, and Luca felt his cock get harder. He was lost to it, whatever they were doing here.

He took her mouth far more aggressively than he had yet. It was like some derangement had gripped him. In the back of his drunken stoned mind, he told himself this wasn't revenge for the kitchen; it wasn't payback for how small she constantly made him feel.

Luca wept and felt himself getting closer.

He couldn't think anymore. He didn't know why he was crying.

He didn't understand anything, other than her wet hot mouth and the noises she was making and the need to keep going. But he had to speak, to make this mean something, if it ever could.

She looked up at him, frowning, questioning.

"Tell me the truth then," he said. "Tell me I didn't rape you before."

"Let's not talk about that *now*..."

"You have to say it." He was panting; his body was roaring at him to keep going. "I mean it."

She rolled her eyes, making it look civilised despite the spit sliding down her chin. "I can say any words I want. It doesn't change reality."

"*Anne.*"

"Fine. It wasn't rape. Okay? *Christ.*"

Luca carried on, crying harder as Anne made choking noises.

CHAPTER FIFTY-ONE

I am writing poetry in a haze of smoke.
Time passes, and a soul dies,
It's too soon tomorrow for sad goodbyes,
The moon watches the sun,
Wild the rabbits run,
Whether we triumph,
Or we come undone.
But now I am watching,
Always in your place,
Look into the mirror, my friend,
And you will see my face.
I am the background in the sigh,
The emptiness in the space.
I am all the ever nobodies,
And the ones who are clawing earth,
I am alone now, and will always be,
Until I leave this place rebirthed.

I look over the words, struggling to focus, wondering if they mean much of anything. There's such a beautiful simple joy in writing things down; I couldn't do anything long-form, I don't think... but this, the direct instantaneousness of poetry. Five minutes of musing, and there's something, an existing thing where before there was only absence.

The emptiness of the page,
Hear the soul rage,
Break out of the cage–

Maybe I'm losing it a bit; maybe I never had it.

Silent listener, I hope you are keeping well in yourself. I know it may seem like I have forgotten you at times, but it's only because it's difficult for me to focus.

Sometimes I wonder if you're Maisie I'm speaking to. But I've never heard your voice. I can feel you there, somewhere close by.

I'm sure this isn't nothing. I'm sure this is poetry, not the blank page.

I hope you're not judging me for looking forward to the meeting with Luca too much. It was two days ago he was here; we're going to meet *this evening*!

The thing is, I'm physically attracted to him, and I'm curious to try sex again. It makes me nervous, don't get me wrong; there's obvious, well, *issues* related to it. Relating to what Kurk did, I mean. But he seems genuine, Luca does. He's a good person.

I could always tell... except with Kurk.

I try writing a story again, but I was right before. It becomes boring, so I write some more poetry.

The sun has set.

It has; it's evening, the world growing quieter.

I have no regrets.

Perhaps this is a wish, but I don't question the pen, as pretentious wannabe Classy Writer Lady as that sounds. I let it guide me; that's the blunt truth, not some affectation. There are no barriers between me and you, silent listener.

I have and always will tell you the truth.
But for one thing...
Your smile,
Forever lost to me,
Taunts invisibly in memory.

CHAPTER FIFTY-TWO

LUCA

"And here I was thinking you were all man..."

Luca looked up through a haze of smoke. His body felt like it was melting into the sofa. They'd had sex three more times that day.

It was evening and they'd been sitting there, smoking and drinking... Even Anne, oh-so precious Anne, had let a cider lead to few puffs on his joint. She was space-eyed, holding something in her hand.

"What?" Luca grunted.

She skipped closer. The alcohol and weed were making her livelier, but Luca wanted to go to sleep. He'd tried to leave several times and she'd giggled softly, telling him, "You can leave if you *have* to. But then I'll be forced to do what *I* have to."

Luca was late for his date with Jess. He wasn't sure what good he'd be to her tonight, but he'd rather see her: the woman he was stealing from. The woman whose life he was going to ruin. Rather be with her than Anne.

"Luca?" Anne was right in front of him, wearing lingerie, her skin reddened here and there from their sex. Luca had no clue where her husband was. Anne had merely laughed and said, *"Don't you worry about it."* The impression Luca got was that Patrick would stay clear for weeks, years if Anne ordered him to.

"What?" he snapped.

She waved the box of Viagra in front of his face. He groaned, shaking his head as he sat up.

"You had me going for a while."

"It's not for you," he said.

"I thought you were a *real* big tough man. Able to get it up even when drunk."

"Give them here."

"Not for me?" She danced away, laughing in that ugly way.

She really was the most confusing person Luca had ever met. He hated her and he wanted to fuck her and he wanted to be anywhere but here.

"But there's one pill missing. And you only got them earlier today. I checked the receipt, tough guy."

Luca tried to laugh it off, but his head was pounding. At some point, Anne had gone out and returned with more booze. She was on vodka and Coke, sipping it with a sick grin on her face every time; it was like she wanted nothing more than to stop, and nothing more than to drink as she glugged it down.

"Fine." He shrugged, sat back. "I took one earlier. I needed it."

Anne recoiled. Luca smiled, enjoyed it. She deserved it. "What's that supposed to mean?"

"Look at you," Luca said, his voice as cruel as he could make it. "If it wasn't for your little video, I'd use you for a quick shag then delete your number. You're a one-time fuck sort of woman, Anne. A halfway attractive older woman you can tell your mates about. You're nothing special."

Luca clawed for his drink, knocked it over. Purple liquid

pooled on the floor, but neither of them cared enough to do anything about it.

Luca grabbed the can, sipping what was left; he stared at her, grinning wider when he realised she had no comeback.

"You've got an average body," he went on. "Pretty fit, yeah. But you can tell your age in places. You do your best to play the part when we're doing kinky stuff, but there's something tragic about you pretending to be a schoolgirl. It's pathetic, honestly. And the way you act with all that wannabe dominatrix stuff..."

His voice was getting louder.

"It's fucking *sad*." He stood abruptly; she lurched back, so melodramatic. "The truth is, you disgusting hag, I'm getting bored of you. Any man would. You're nothing but a classic damaged slut. *Oh, somebody diddled me so I call you Daddy.*"

Spit was flying from Luca's mouth as he walked over to her, waving his hands, shouting right in her face. "Without Viagra it'd be *impossible* to fuck you."

Anne's eye was twitching. Luca had never seen anybody so angry.

And there was something else.

He regretted everything he'd said, hating that she'd made him go there– no, *he'd* gone there.

He swayed, returning to his seat.

Anne sat in the opposite armchair. She was staring into space, with no emotion in her expression at all. Luca almost wanted her to shout at him, but she just sat there.

"Do you want another drink?" Luca asked after a few minutes; it felt far longer, sitting there with her shell-shocked look, and Luca thinking about the things he'd said, the things he'd never want Izzy to hear.

But Anne wasn't recording. Luca had checked, and she'd laughed; she always did.

"Sure," she said softly.

Luca went into the kitchen and made her one, bringing it back. She took it wordlessly. Luca sat and finished his cider.

Anne took a few sips of her drink and then looked over at him. "You're not a good person. I don't want to argue, and I don't want a discussion about it... but a good person wouldn't even think to say the things you said to me. A good person would know how downright despicable it is to *imagine* such evil, sexist things, much less say them."

Luca opened his mouth, but she went on.

"To categorise a woman's sexuality like that, in such *cynical* terms. And you, big tough man Luca, who cares so much for his little sister. I know why you really care about her."

Luca's fist tightened, causing his empty cider can to crush loudly. Anne sneered at it. "Ooh, did I touch a nerve?"

"I thought you didn't want a discussion."

"About the awful, ugly, untrue things you said, yes. But we're not talking about that. We're talking about how much you like to fuck your baby sister."

"I warned you about her!"

Luca leapt to his feet, sprung across the living room. A haze fell over his eyes and all he knew, all which existed for him was to hurt. To cause agony, of the worst kind. He was panting like a goddamn animal.

He stopped, standing over her chair, to find her staring up at him.

"You know what they say." Anne folded her legs. "The man who protests too much... You're not exactly helping your incest kiddy-diddling case."

"You're so sick." He bit down so hard his teeth hurt. "You're broken."

"I bet she gets *real* excited when your parents go on holiday..."

Luca had to step away. He was going to do something very stupid. Anne didn't understand how dangerous this was, provoking a trained fighter with alcohol buzzing through his system. It was an insane position for her to put him in.

"I'm going for a piss."

He turned, walked away. Then her hand was on his arm. She made to pull him around, but he stood there, not moving. "Let go, Anne."

"Run away from the fight like a coward."

"I don't want a fight."

"Says the one who started it. Pathetic."

"Let go of my arm."

"Or what?" She dug her nails in a little. "Are you going to take more Viagra and rape me?"

"Such a sad old woman."

He shrugged her hand away, and then something exploded on the wall next to him. He looked down to find her glass, Coke spilling everywhere. Luca ducked his head and strode from the room, and then Anne started yelling. "You're a fucking loser! A fucking nobody! You're disgusting! Pig! Fucking coward!"

Luca was shaking as he locked the bathroom door behind him. He gave the door a rattle, to make sure it was locked, then walked over to the toilet. He sat heavily and stared into space, shaking, hugging his knees because he felt so cold.

He flinched as she raged in the next room; she was throwing things against the walls, smashing the place up, and suddenly Luca hated this: not only what she was doing, but *him*, the person he became reflected in her.

Before he could think about it, he took out his phone. He rang Jess quickly. He didn't care, wouldn't dwell on the video.

"Luca?" Jess's voice was tight. "I thought it was a joke after all; I thought you weren't coming."

"We're going to steal your money."

More crashing in the next room. Luca was crying, but he more heard it than felt it. It was like his voice belonged to somebody else. He knew this was it, the right thing, and he couldn't let himself think about anything else.

"What?" Jess whispered.

"There's no Uncle Stellan. Anne's blackmailing me to go along with it because she wants to steal your money."

"Luca." Jess's tautness had snapped, her voice tremoring. "I don't understand. This doesn't make any sense."

"I'm sorry." He sobbed, choking on it; he couldn't seem to stop. "She came to my house with a recording of the meeting we had. In the barn. Remember?"

"But there was no–"

"There *was*. We've been lying to you. *I've* been lying to you. But I'm done. I don't care what she does to me. She's poison."

"You must be–"

"Who do you trust more, Jess, me or Anne? Who do you *know* more?"

"You, Luca," she said, and then paused. "Yes, you."

"I swear, I'm telling the truth. She's been... she's been rough with me. And it's made me into a prick. We had a huge fight. I'm surprised you can't hear her going nuts."

"What's she doing?"

"Do you believe me?" Luca said.

"I hate you for this."

"I know you do."

"If you're telling the truth, or if you're lying, I hate you for it."

"I know. But I'm telling you. Don't give her any money. *She's* the abuser. I haven't seen her hurt her husband, but she treats him like shit. I'm there now, in his house; she told him to get lost and he did, no questions. Would an abuser do that?"

242

"And she has a video of you."

"She cut it together to make it seem like I'm defending myself for rape. I'm so sorry... *fuck*. I don't know."

"It's okay, Luca," Jess said softly.

He covered his mouth, another sob coming out. His throat hurt from all the crying. He could feel it, especially his cheeks stinging. He wanted it all to end.

"Have you been drinking?" Jess asked.

"Yeah. Can you tell?"

She laughed softly. "Yes. You should stick to weed, young man. Or you won't be able to fuck me."

Luca laughed through the tears, feeling hopeful for a brief moment. Despite Anne shouting something in the next room – maybe she was tearing his bag apart – he didn't care. Just for a second.

"How can you forgive me?"

"We're friends."

"But Anne is..."

"You asked me if I trust you more. Obviously I do. We've spent so much time together, really a staggering amount when you stop to think about it, at least by my terms. I believe you. It makes sense. And the truth is..."

"What?"

"I don't remember what happened when she left the woods. Her driving away, any of it. I blacked out."

"Fuck's *sake*, Jess."

"I know." She sighed. "I know. I should say sorry too. My plan, Luca, my original plan was for you to..."

She trailed off, like she couldn't say it.

"I know," Luca told her. "And I forgive you too."

Suddenly the bathroom door made a loud cracking noise, vibrating in the frame. Anne's voice was more vicious than he'd ever heard it. *"Open this door, fucking coward!"*

"Can you hear that?" Luca said.

"Yes," Jess replied. "I can. I'm coming to get you."

"I'm going to slit Izzy's cunt throat and make you watch!"

"Jess," Luca whispered. "What should I do?"

"I can't believe she'd say that," Jess said.

Anne went on, and Jess groaned down the phone. "If you can get out of the house, do that. If not, wait in there. Maybe I can speak to her."

"She's not who you think she is."

The slamming stopped. Anne's voice changed. "Luca, are you on the phone?"

"Don't hang up," Jess said. "Put your phone in your pocket or something. I'm leaving. It's going to take me forty-five or so minutes."

Luca tucked his phone into his pocket and stood.

"I was talking to myself," he snapped at Anne, opening the door.

She raised her hand; it was shaking, like the rest of her. She'd shredded a book and paper was scattered all over the hallway. Several frames lay on the floor, broken glass in them.

"I don't believe you."

"That's your problem. I'm leaving."

"Leaving?" She was doing her civilised voice, probably because she knew he might be recording, or still on the phone. But it was pathetic; Jess had already heard the real Anne. "Why?"

"Why," Luca repeated bluntly. As if that was even a question. "See you around."

"You might want to think about a certain film..."

They stared at each other in the hallway, Anne looking ill with booze and weed, and almost a little regretful. Or maybe Luca was letting his imagination go crazy, thinking she could regret anything.

"I don't care," he lied.

"Please don't be like this, baby. Please. I didn't mean to get angry."

"Jess knows. She heard it all. So drop the act."

CHAPTER FIFTY-THREE

PATRICK

Patrick sat in the pub, taking another sip of his pint. There were a group of men to his left, all patting each other on the back, discussing a bet they'd placed. He took his phone from the bar and flipped it over, checking his messages.

He yawned, took another sip, and ignored the tremor in his chest. His body was a mess. He should've been at the gym, in the sauna or something.

But mostly, he wanted sleep. He wondered what Anne was doing. He wondered if he needed to book a hotel. She hadn't given him any details, only telling him to stay out of the house until she rang him.

He finished his pint, thinking of when they'd met, a classic bombshell captures a dinosaur scenario, and the real love there, and the slow changing of it, and the signs which were only signs when viewed from the unknowable years ahead.

CHAPTER FIFTY-FOUR

"*Are you really going to wear that lame thing?*" Anne says, as I listen through speakerphone, driving through the night.

Her voice is insanely convincing. I find myself wondering if perhaps Luca is exaggerating a few things. Maybe they had a bad argument and he's twisting the facts.

But I could hear the genuine pain in his voice; I've so rarely witnessed men crying like that. Even hearing it felt raw.

I drive, following the satnav, remembering something Luca said to me weeks ago. "It's one small chunk after the next, life, Jess... and the trick is to make each one feel like its own story."

The drive was chapter one; the house was the final chapter two.

Whether Luca exaggerated or not, I need to get to him. But it's difficult to remember the woman who'd screamed such awful things when this Anne speaks. "*You look like a bit of a dork, like a wannabe businessman, with that thing in your ear.*"

The sound quality changes, Luca's voice coming through clearer. I recognise it as his headset pairing with his phone.

"*Jess, you can talk now if you want. I can hear you, but she can't.*"

My headlights are cutting across the dark roads surrounding the city.

"Leave," I tell him. "We can sort all this out later."

"*I am. Anne– don't be stupid. Give me my bag.*"

"*I don't see why you're treating me like this.*"

"*She heard you shouting at me. She heard what you said.*"

"*What I said?*" Anne laughs. "*You're the one who said any woman who enjoys sex must've been raped as a child.*"

"*I didn't say that!*" Luca roars.

"Luca." I drive a little faster, trying to keep my breathing steady. "Luca, leave! Forget about your bag."

"*My stuff's in there,*" Luca snaps. "*Anne, seriously, it's over. We're not stealing Jess's money anymore. I never should've agreed to that to begin with.*"

"*I told you I never wanted to do that,*" Anne says, and I find myself wondering. "*It's a horrible idea. I wish you wouldn't talk about it.*"

"*She knows your uncle doesn't exist. And you can lie all you want, but Jess will find out if she wants. She used to be a journalist.*"

"*Used to be,*" Anne says derisively.

I replay it over and over, hundreds of times in the space of a second. Hearing her tone, the dismissiveness of it, the superiority. I think of Luca, of this stranger smoking weed outside a car rental place, of his smile and the way he stares right into my eyes and soul when he speaks.

"Used to be," I say softly.

"*Yeah, Jess. That's her. The real Anne.*"

"*I mean it's great,*" Anne goes on in her bubbly tone. "*Maybe she'll be able to dig up some information that can help Stellan.*"

"He doesn't exist. You're a liar. You're abusing your husband. And we both know what you do to me."

I pause at a turning, waiting as a driver's beams glare at me, far too much light flooding the car. I pull down the sun visor and keep driving.

"What I do to you... You're either deluded or just cruel."

"Whatever. My bag. Anne."

"Luca," I say, "seriously, leave the bag. This doesn't sound good. Any of it. I want you two away from each other."

Suddenly I wish for Korey, pray for Korey, and remember that in-between spot when I met Luca before he met Anne. I want to go back there.

"It's my bag. It's my fucking stuff in there."

"Are you going to hit me again, Luca?"

"You're transparent. It's sad. She heard you and you're still lying like..."

Like she believes it, I fill in silently, gaze flitting to the satnav as their voices fill the car.

I'm a good driver, with how much whizzing around I do. But my concentration is straining here; all of me wants to leap through the phone, do something, make it stop.

I am Maisie, racing through the terrifying blackness; maybe that was it all along.

Not Anne, *me*.

Can that be true–

I scream as I veer around the squirrel, focusing quickly, righting the car as the tail tries to whip out. I breathe steadily and try not to panic, but I'm not going fast enough.

"Anne–"

"Leave me alo–"

"Anne–"

Luca yells.

Something crashes.

There's a rattling noise as the Bluetooth headset breaks.

It's crackling and I can hear some of it. Their voices clashing, something else making a loud noise of destruction, mayhem over there, complete chaos, as I struggle to pay attention on this unlit winding road.

"Luca," I say, tears sliding down my face and over my lips. "Get out of there."

CHAPTER FIFTY-FIVE

LUCA

There was something terrible happening to the side of his head.

In his ear.

It happened again, and his world shook. He was forgetting his own name, and he wished he hadn't smoked or drunk that night.

Deeper into his ear, and he couldn't hear the noise, but he could feel the sound of it, like boots in sticky autumn mud.

He was fighting; some part of him was, his hands spasming, but there was no real battle in that.

He could smell the pain, and taste the hopelessness.

CHAPTER FIFTY-SIX

I pull up outside the house, this gorgeous magnetic place, this sacred site.

As I jog over to the gate, I think of the first time I was here, climbing the fence, before I met Luca, before I was *me*, the person I am now: before the weed, or at least this fling with it.

Headlights come to life on the other side of the house. I can see the wide ends of them, clawing through the dark in deep yellow. The lights get brighter and closer, finally turning and settling on me.

Then they go off.

I try to see who's driving, but they're clothed in darkness, and I get the sense it's intentional.

"Anne?" I shout. "Luca, is that you?"

The car door flies open and Anne springs out. I can tell it's her by her silhouette. She gets closer, and all at once I see Maisie again: storming around in a temper tantrum, a wonderful rage.

Anne gets closer, comes into the street's light.

Where is that scar on her lip, the one which reminded me of Maisie? I wonder if it was ever there.

She looks tired, eyes red, with damp hair as though she's

recently showered. Her clothes are clean; they seem too big for her somehow. Or maybe it's how shrunken she is.

"Where's Luca?"

She's finding it hard to look at me. I didn't bother with the mask or anything.

And suddenly I hate her for it. Because if Luca's telling the truth, it means she'd have no problem lying to me, faking moments, tricking me into believing I'm worth something.

Anger boils and demons spill out, and my head gets groggy as the call to blood booms like a war drum.

"Anne?"

She sneers – an out-and-out sneer, a bona fide look of genuine disgust. Then she replaces it, or tries to. She's clearly drunk.

"He left." She pouts. "I was going to look for him."

"You're too drunk to drive."

"You don't know anything about me."

Something in me snaps; I'm not sure what. But one second I'm staring at her, the next I've slammed my hands against the bars of the gate. I've brought my face close and I'm raising my voice. "I'm going to ask you something. Answer me honestly."

"I'll always be–"

"Do you have an Uncle Stellan?"

She looks at me for a long time. And I see it, the same way I would with Maisie when she was younger, considering a lie, wondering how little truth she can get away with.

But Maisie grew out of it.

"No," she says.

"Did you cut your own belly?"

She gasps. "No, never! Some of what Luca said was true, but not all of it. He was drunk. He wanted to hurt me. We had an argument."

"So why lie about your uncle?"

253

"I wanted your help, but I didn't know how to ask," she wails, and there's something off about it, like her performance is faltering.

I think of right at the end of the phone call, the crashing, that awful noise as his headset broke: shattered in his ear. Please let that not be true. But that's what it sounded like, the headset breaking... and why would that happen, if not through violence?

"Tell me where Luca is."

She shakes her head, and I remember the run-ins I've had over the years. Watching people isn't always safe work. There are monsters down alleyways, and not just me. *Ha ha fucking ha*. But it's the truth.

"Anne, I need to explain something," I tell her, fighting that pathetic shudder in my voice. "You're drunk. If you try to stop me, you're going to get yourself hurt."

The sneer returns. "Stop you from *what*?"

"I want to check Luca isn't there." I gesture to the street. "Because that's his car. And we both know it's his car."

I'm not sure I've ever read Anne correctly, but I am now.

She flinches, looks toward the car she was driving before I arrived. I almost cry again, because I know I'm right.

"I heard you shouting. And I heard his Bluetooth headset break."

"That thing." A surreal smile slithers seductively onto her face, then vanishes. "I don't know what to tell you. We had an argument and he left."

I look up and down the street, quiet, only us.

"Where's your husband?" I ask.

"He's working late."

"Okay then. I'm going to come onto the property and look around."

"You're *not*."

I walk over to my car, reach into the glovebox, and take out a heavy combat knife I ordered online. It's the sort they use in the military, completely illegal, almost a machete in its length.

Gripping it hard, I walk up to the gate, softly pushing it open.

"This is ridiculous," Anne says. "You can't do this."

"Then call the police," I say, sidestepping toward the car as she trails after me; it's like we're doing some alien dance.

When she gives me more expressional hints, I keep moving. She's telling me where to go by where she wants me *not* to go, looking at the car then back at me, at the car again, mostly clothed in darkness.

Again, I remember the crackling of the headset, and I note her recently showered self, and her tired eyes, and how wired and weird she's behaving.

I never knew her, silent listener.

I have never known anybody except for my daughter, not even myself.

It's Anne's car, looking how it did in the woods, except for a blotch of something on the boot. Keeping my knife arm primed, I slowly take my phone from my pocket, turn on the torch, and guide it back and forth over the car.

There's the blood, proving my instincts right, my current ones, when I remove all thought of Anne being the woman I thought she was. When I let myself really *look*.

"Open the boot."

"Jess—"

"Open the boot or I'm going to stab you."

She looks back at the house, and I laugh meanly. I laugh like Kurk would. What an effective weapon it is; how endlessly grand he must've felt.

"Or run if you want, and I'll open the boot. Either way, I'm going to see what's inside."

She narrows her eyes at me, then turns as if to look back at the house—

I leap forward, unthinking.

Grabbing a big chunk of her hair, I bring the knife to her throat. I can feel her hair tugging against her scalp as I make my grip tighter. I give into this feeling and slam her head against the boot, almost collapsing myself, the violence is so shocking.

She bounces off it; she would fall if I didn't pull her back into position.

"Don't make me ask you again."

Her gaze flits to the knife.

I step back, ready to leap at her if she tries anything.

"Please don't hurt me." Anne sounds so young, so Maisie-ish, as she opens the boot and steps back. "I didn't mean it."

Keeping the knife aimed at her, I kneel down and carefully pick up my phone. It must've fallen to the ground during the scuffle.

Turning my torch on, I guide it over Luca's corpse.

It's a miracle she was able to get him in here, his legs folded beneath him, his arms unnaturally crushed under his chest.

She stamped on his head repeatedly, it looks like, or at least struck him countless times; his Bluetooth headset is part of his skull, assaulted into his flesh. One eye, entirely swollen with blood, stares as if begging for me to remove it.

Anne makes a dash for the house, and I watch her go.

I know what I have to do.

"Run!" I shout after her. "But when I leave, you finish this job. You get him away. You take him as far away from here as you can."

Nobody can find him: not the police.

Anne has to go free. She has to wait for me.

Walking over to Luca, I reach into the car, softly trailing my hand across his mashed face, his pulverised cheeks. She must've taken him by surprise – and the alcohol – and the drama of it all... And once she started, she couldn't stop.

I try to remove his headset, but it makes his head wobble, so I leave it in place. Then I start to cry. "I'm so sorry, Luca."

CHAPTER FIFTY-SEVEN

PATRICK

Patrick was at the sink, rinsing the dishes as Anne stood at the window. She was tense, a glass of vodka in her hand, staring into the semi-darkness as if searching for answers. Patrick didn't even know what the bloody questions were; he felt like he never had.

Two weeks previously, when Anne had ordered Patrick to stay away, she'd sent him a text.

> Don't come home until tomorrow evening.

No explanation, and Patrick didn't ask for one. He wondered if he'd ever be the sort of man who *could* ask. When he finally returned, the house had been unusually clean, reeking of cleaning chemicals. He wondered if she'd been doing drugs, or had held some wild party.

He didn't mention the vodka; the not-drinking never lasted long with Anne.

He rinsed the final dishes and placed them in the washer, setting it to cycle. Imagining walking up behind his wife, gently cradling her shoulders, he turned away and made to walk into the living room.

"Wait," she said coldly.

Patrick froze in place. His heart felt faulty, beating way too hard. It had been getting worse lately. He wondered if that summer flu had had anything to do with it... but no, *flu* couldn't do that.

A heeled shoe to the chest – ribcage problems – heart problems – he couldn't breathe...

He needed to calm down; he needed to stop. Anne was talking and he wasn't listening.

It was the worst moment he could've chosen to be absent-minded. She abruptly stopped, her hand trembling on her vodka glass. She walked toward him and nodded to the hallway.

"Bedroom."

"Anne..." His chest was really in a lot of pain. "Please..."

"Bed-fucking-room, *now*."

He turned, head bowed, and together they walked up the stairs. He tried to do it slowly; she laughed in that mean way, sensing he was delaying, but she didn't make him walk quicker.

In the bedroom, he thought about how he'd wash his hands afterward, at the sink, and the blood would swirl down the plughole. He thought about how she would come down, and it would be like magic; there she was, his civilised beautiful wife. She wouldn't hurt a fly.

"Go on," she said, as she went to the dresser and knelt down. She reached to the back and took out the satchel. It looked like something a barber might carry his scissors in.

Patrick made to grab the foldout chair from near the wardrobe, but she tutted. "No, sit on the stool. My vanity unit. Are you *stupid*? It's right there."

Patrick had been about to say it was a bit low. He was getting lots of aches and pains. But her tone hurried him along.

She took the foldout chair instead, and sat right in front of him, staring into his eyes as she unzipped the satchel.

"I want you to know, you earned this," she said, her voice all wavy with vodka. "Because you're not a man. You never were one. A real man who knows how to support his wife, how to make her happy, but all you care about is yourself. All you care about is your shitty job."

As she spoke, she took out the three-part riding crop and began screwing it together.

"What are you going to tell your oh-so important friends, you pathetic old man? That you've started boxing again?"

"Maybe..." Patrick blinked; there were tears in his eyes.

"Maybe *what*?" she snapped, clicking the final piece into place.

"Maybe I'll tell them I started boxing, yes. Or that I was doing some gardening."

"Whatever."

Anne abruptly stood.

Patrick put his hands out, knuckles up.

Tricksy was running ahead of him, tail wagging, and Laura was just ahead of the dog. Laura was so little and so bright and full of happiness; the sun bounced off her hair, and then Tricksy caught her and they fell down in the grass.

Patrick kept running, but his legs were fixed in place; his sister and his dog were getting further away.

He sat up, panting, in bed, with soaked sheets beneath him, groaning as his hip gave a sharp jolt.

Placing his feet on the floor, he leaned over, wondering what he'd been dreaming about. It had already left him. He didn't sense Anne in the room, but that was nothing new. After... *after*, she often slept downstairs, or in the spare room. It was like she couldn't stand the sight of him.

He needed a glass of water, and he was tempted to change the sheets. The digital clock told him it was half past two in the morning. He stood – painfully – and cracked the window open.

He normally remembered to bring a glass up there, but he'd forgotten.

Walking downstairs, his eyes bleary with sleep, he noticed something wrong with the carpet. The main light was off, but a lamp was lit... had Anne put in a new carpet? There was an odd pattern on it, sort of abstract, flecks of red here and there. It was on the stairs too, and there was a smear on the wall.

There was a smear on the wall.

He stopped, stared at it, stared.

There is a red smear on the wall, his thoughts told him, very slowly, and he felt his heart quicken; it was enough to cause him pain.

From the living room, he heard muffled groaning.

He went inside, his head getting light; there were more smears and more patterns and he knew what it was, when he saw her. It took his mind seconds as he gazed, to make sense of it.

Anne was naked, tied to a chair, her hands tied together in her lap and her feet tied to each other, and then rope went from her feet to the chair, holding them tautly in place. There was more rope around her midriff, keeping her upright.

A blood-soaked rag was stuffed into her mouth. Her pretty blonde hair was matted with blood.

Looking closer, Patrick's belly churned; he was paralysed as his gaze fixated on her hands, her missing fingers.

She shouted something, but Patrick couldn't hear.

He'd fallen and he was finding it difficult to make sense of anything.

And to breathe; he silently laughed at that, somewhere in his head, as he wondered which was more important. Sense or breath.

Somebody stepped over him. The figure was slim. He wondered if the person was a man or a woman. The shape of them looked too small to be Theo.

"If you make another noise," the voice said. It was a woman's, upper class, and so calm Patrick thought for a second this was some elaborate gameshow or something. A horror reality TV show. No way would a real killer sound so calm. "I'm going to stick this knife in your useless mouth and move it around a bunch. Nod if you understand."

Anne must've nodded. Patrick couldn't see; the slim figure was partially blocking her. He was finding it difficult to keep his eyes open. There was a massive weight on his chest.

"No screaming," the woman said, as she reached for the rag in Anne's mouth and slowly pulled it out, stepping aside as if to give Patrick a better view.

But really, it was like Patrick wasn't even there. He was nothing but an onlooker to his own life; that was all he'd ever been.

Anne was panting, sounding delirious with pain, her eyes opening and closing as though she was fighting unconsciousness; she would've fallen forward if not for the ropes around her middle. "You have to get him an ambulance. He's having a heart attack."

"How simple you must find it, amongst regular people," the woman went on calmly. "*Acta, non verba.* But you have always used words, haven't you, Anne? You want to use words here, to save yourself, by making me believe you care about your husband? Again, actions, my dear sweet Anne, not words. You were never Maisie."

"P-puh-please." She sounded like she was spitting blood. "Help him. He needs an ambulance."

"As if you care. Do you really think I'm going to fall for that? Okay, Anne, let's see how much you care... let's put it to the test..."

The woman knelt next to Patrick and grabbed him around the throat; Anne and Patrick were staring at each other. There was something in her eyes; it was a look he recognised from whenever he'd failed in the marriage.

It was like she was silently screaming at him, *Why didn't you wake up? Why didn't you protect me?*

"I told you I'd kill him for you," the woman said, her nails digging into Patrick's neck. "Look, you're getting what you want. Like you always do."

Patrick felt the knife go in his side, a sharp punching fire like he'd never felt.

She stabbed him again, and it was fleshy and wet; she kept going, slicing up and down his belly, lacerating his flesh, until the pain was too much and his eyes were too heavy.

He was conscious of shouting in agony; conscious too of a surprisingly strong hand over his mouth, mostly trapping the noise. But it all felt so far away.

Even his body's spasming, the lurching as he impotently attempted to defend himself; it was distant, as though it wasn't his concern.

Anne was looking intently at what the killer did.

Right before Patrick's eyes closed, he thought he saw Anne smile.

But she wouldn't. Not in his final moments. Not even Anne.

CHAPTER FIFTY-EIGHT

ANNE

J ess was covered in blood, and when she smiled, her face shivered and distorted; Anne's vision was wavering as her body tried to force her to pass out.

But she was stronger than the Bad Place and stronger than the useless mess of blood and weakness on the floor; Patrick had somehow slept through Jess dragging Anne down the stairs, stabbing her, forcing her into this room where she wrestled her into the chair.

Anne had screamed at least twice before Jess got the rag into her mouth.

And yet Patrick had slept, dreaming of God only knew what... certainly not *Anne*.

She was strong; she hadn't passed out, even when Jess began lopping off fingers with a sharp knife. She *wouldn't* pass out.

"What a surprise," Jess said, in that calm voice. "You don't give a single fuck he's dead, do you? In fact, you'd prefer it... if you somehow got out alive, it would be perfect for you. What a victim that would make you."

"J-Jess, p-please..."

Each word was torture. She could feel her amputated fingers throbbing; she was curling them tightly, which was impossible... she could see a few of them littered on the floor. But she felt it anyway.

"What a hero," Jess went on.

"P-please."

Jess strode over to her. She was like an animal, fixed on her task. Anne stared in horrified wonder at the pit of gore where her husband's belly had been.

"Open your mouth."

"P-please–"

"Now."

Anne did as Jess said, and Jess shoved the rag in, pushed it so far back it choked Anne. She felt her head getting light again, but she wouldn't black out.

There had to be an escape.

What would your daughter say? Anne wanted to scream, but there was nothing.

Jess stepped away, laughing darkly. "How badly you want to argue. To plead your case. That's what you do, all of you, Narcissus staring into the pool. Luca didn't deserve to die."

Anne tried to scream again, but then Jess hit her so hard the chair fell sideways. Anne's head bounced off the floor and she felt it leaking: her blood, her skull, it all felt so physical and *feelable* in a way it shouldn't have been.

"I hope I don't remember this," Jess said.

Anne stared at Patrick. His mouth was opening and closing slowly. It looked like he was trying to say *I love you.* Anne couldn't be sure.

Then Jess knelt, blocking her view.

Anne gasped, choking on the gag, as Jess grabbed a big fistful of her hair and brought the knife to her throat. "Sometimes, I know I can't remember certain things. I have to lock it all away. I think you understand that, unless you were lying about being born in a cult."

Anne hadn't been lying. *Keep sweet keep sweet keep sweet...* flickering videotapes were trying to swallow her, and Anne wondered if it was Hell beckoning.

"But I can't be sure. I might remember this. I might remember killing Patrick and..." Jess began to cry, big gasping sobs; it was like repressed agony burst through the calmness. "But I didn't do it. I didn't set my house on fire. I didn't plan on grabbing Maisie quickly, and leaving Kurk passed out from whisky in bed. He didn't wake, find me doing it. We didn't waste precious time having a fight as Maisie burned to death in her room. None of that happened."

Jess, Anne tried to say, but then Jess stabbed the knife into Anne's neck.

It slipped in so sharp, and then Jess did it again. She became feral, slicing, poking Anne full of holes.

Anne screamed and thrashed about, the chair legs making wooden noises against the floor, the rag trapping whatever Anne's final words might've been.

CHAPTER FIFTY-NINE

I stand on the other side of the clearing, watching the motorhome burn in the darkness. As the flames flicker and I come to terms with my next logical step – get as far away from here as possible, pray I'm not found and forced to spend my life inside a cage – I wonder why I killed Patrick too.

The murders are lost to me, as unknowable as the time Anne emerged from the woods. There's a hole there, except for the very end, when I closed the door behind me and ran down the path.

But the hole isn't complete. There are snippets. I remember Patrick on the floor, a crimson vignette of death. I know I murdered him as certainly as I know I took Anne's life.

It's more like I don't *want* to remember, so I don't. I wonder if that's the case with so much else, if I've been blocking things out more willingly than I'd care to admit.

How can I know without peeling it all away?

That's something I'll never do.

The police have my DNA; I have to assume this to be the case, since I can't remember the crime scene. Unless I was especially careful, they have it. People will have seen Anne and Luca together, and me and Luca.

I'm not sure how this will end. I can't know.

Walking across the clearing, twigs stabbing my bare feet, I step closer to the flames; I feel their heat, let them lick at my nakedness. I've stripped off all the clothes from earlier, scrubbed myself raw.

The flames get hotter, more welcoming, more destructive as I bask in them, letting them wash away all of it, the mess of what happened, of where watching got me.

No more watching, I tell myself. *Never again.*

That Patrick situation really is a sore point for me, silent listener. I can only assume he tried to stand up for Anne. I was forced to defend myself.

I never intended to harm him.

Fighting the pain, the memories, I move closer to the flames.

Later, I'm driving down a country road. A house sits on a hill. The yellow lights sing out over the darkness, calling to me.

It's been a week since the murders: since I fled the city. I shouldn't risk this.

But the lights, and the promise of something which isn't *me*...

I pull up at the side of the road.

THE END

ACKNOWLEDGEMENTS

I would like to thank the whole Bloodhound team, and particularly Betsy and Fred Freeman, Tara Lyons, and Morgen Bailey, my ever-vigilant editor.

I'd also like to pay a special thanks to my friends and family.

As always, I owe unending gratitude to my wife, Krystle, without whom I never would have finished anything even remotely publishable... so you can thank or blame her, as the case may be.

This note wouldn't be complete without thanking you, the reader. I understand my work can be polarising, extreme, strange... some might pick different words: terrible, unacceptably bizarre, etc. Whatever the case, I thank you, sincerely and passionately.

At heart, I'm still a kid walking into a careers meeting with lofty dreams of putting pen to paper, of making a living from it. Without you, none of this would be possible.

A NOTE FROM THE PUBLISHER

Thank you for reading this book. If you enjoyed it please do consider leaving a review on Amazon to help others find it too.

We hate typos. All of our books have been rigorously edited and proofread, but sometimes mistakes do slip through. If you have spotted a typo, please do let us know and we can get it amended within hours.

info@bloodhoundbooks.com

Printed in Great Britain
by Amazon

17149544R00160